ISBN:
ISBN-13: 978-1508927129

.

Acknowledgements

Thank you to my wife, Lisa, and our children Jonah and Sonja for being the brightest lights of this stunning earthly existence.

Thank you to my parents, big brother, and two little sisters (and their families) for making me who I am.

Thank you to the boys of Apartment 118 and the boys of Ansley Drive - your friendships are the cornerstone of my foundation as a man.

Thank you to Phillip Oliver for a beautiful cover design and to Lindsay Hicks for trudging through my inadequacies with the English language as my copy editor.

Thank you to the nearly thirty beta readers who gave me honest and helpful feedback.

Thank you to Jeff Goins for giving me the courage to call myself a writer.

Thank you to the beautiful people of DBC for giving me a place to do what I love, with the people I love, for the One who first loved me.

And thank you to the Professor. You've been teaching me something new every day my entire lifetime.

I am eternally grateful.

For Sonja Jane Larson.

I remember you.

Chapter One

"You never even worried with Jane, whether your hand was sweaty or not. All you knew was, you were happy. You really were." - J.D. Salinger

Marty Drake remembered Jane Carson.

That was the problem.

Standing on the front step of a strange house in a neighborhood he'd never been to, sweaty palms and racing heart rate, he remembered her with every cell and synapse in his being.

"Did you pack the items in the box as you were instructed?"

The tone of the question wasn't warm, but it wasn't harsh, either. Business-like. Matter-of-fact. The person standing in the door of the house seemed more like an apparition than a man. There appeared to be no light coming from inside. Only shadows, mystery.

"Yes," Marty answered. Now becoming fully aware of how preposterous it all was. Did he really want to do this? Was it even possible? If it *were* possible, what about the risks? Was it safe? And why would he put his life and future in the hands of someone he only met yesterday? Why was he even here?

Marty Drake remembered her.

That was why he was here.

Standing there, he could sense his own desperation warring against what might be better judgment. Better judgment was losing. Sure, he'd love for it to be different. But he had tried everything else. Everything else had failed.

There seemed no other way.

Marty shifted his weight back and forth on the concrete doorstep. This was even more difficult than he thought it would be. Suddenly it felt like he was giving away treasure, like he was giving away his heart. Yes, it *was* his heart he was giving away. But maybe it had to go. He gathered his courage, like someone picking up loose clothes on his way to the laundry room. He extended his arms forward, hands holding the box that contained almost everything that had become precious to him.

It wasn't a large box, didn't need to be. It was just a standard storage container, about the size a copy paper box with a removable top and holes on either side for carrying. The lid was secured with red duct tape along each side and across the top. The material, both the box and the tape, was provided for him by the person standing in the doorway, packed and secured to his exact specifications. With its contents, it was less than three pounds.

Less than three pounds, yet the weight of the world.

The person in the doorway studied him intently, looking for any sign of doubt, of retreat. "Are you certain this is the path you want to take?" He probed. And for a moment there was no answer. They just stared at each other in the twilight, a light mist of rain beginning to settle on Marty's hair and skin, moisture gradually gathering on the top of the box. He looked down, unable to withstand the penetrating gaze, stalling, avoiding eye contact, staring at the laces on his athletic shoes.

After a few more seconds of delay, Marty focused on his feet as they shuffled nervously toward the door. He extended the box further forward, and felt the light burden shift from his arms to the waiting hands of the shadowy figure in the house. The transfer felt like a surgery of sorts, like an abrupt removal of something that had taken root. Like electricity passing from one object to another. "I'm certain," he said, in a way-less-than-certain voice. Almost always, letting go of something requires much more effort than grabbing hold of it.

As soon as Marty released the box, he experienced a brief moment of panic. Like a mother who puts her newborn in the hands of a teenage babysitter. His instinct was to reach out, forcefully snatch it back, and push the man down. To sprint away, far away, as far as his feet and legs and heart and lungs and will would take him. He would tear open the box and hold its contents in his hands, pore over them with his eyes, clutch them close to his chest. And he would feel…comfortable, safe. A stark contrast to what he was feeling now.

Anxiety. Fear. Panic.

Marty reached forward, as if starting to take the box back. The person holding it did not flinch - he would not put up a fight, would not force Marty to go through with it. This was free will, no compulsion or manipulation whatsoever. A choice. A path. Maybe a second chance. The lack of response calmed Marty and his arms fell back to his sides. Resigned. Surrendered.

The figure in the door placed the box under his left arm, turned around and began slowly walking down the hallway. "Follow me," he called over his shoulder. Marty, having a brief sensation he was being watched from somewhere outside the house, looked over his shoulder before crossing over the threshold. He began following the man down the corridor of the house. It didn't seem nearly as dark inside, now that he was out of the fading daylight and his eyes began to adjust. But it wasn't brightly lit, either. The hallway seemed to stretch on, longer than seemed possible for a house that size. Marty kept his eyes down, watching one foot fall in front of the other on the faded brown carpet, controlling his breathing, steeling himself for what was about to happen.

What *was* about to happen?

As he trailed a few steps behind, his gaze went up to the box. He still had the urge to grab it and take it back, to run. But he knew what was inside must be left behind, put away, destroyed. They neared the end of the hallway and the man in front turned to the left through the opening that led to a larger room. As he did, Marty looked at the box. His eyes focused in on what was written on the bottom corner. It was written in black marker, in all caps, in his handwriting.

It was just one word.

JANE.

Chapter Two

"The Past can be a nice place to visit, but it's a terrible place to live." - Unknown

Some memories seem more like a dream you once had - too good to be true. Some memories are like a tear in the fabric of the soul - ever-widening with wear and the passage of time.

Marty Drake's heart was coming apart at the seams.

He was at a bus stop about a mile from the coffee shop where he worked. Seated on the top of the bench, his feet resting on the seat. Rain was falling, though he seemed oblivious to it.

No cover. No rain gear. No umbrella.

His arms were resting on his legs, hands clasped together, head hanging down. The rain was steady, with oversize drops that landed upon him, assaulting his clothes and skin. The water rolled down his shirt across the arch of his back. It crept forward over his head, the closely-cut hair offering little resistance.

A car zoomed past occasionally, churning up a wake. It had been at least ten minutes since a bus had stopped, coming and going without any exchange of passengers. Marty never looked up, but he sort-of envied the people in cars or on the bus. He didn't know their destination, but they were in motion.

At least they were going somewhere.

Marty wasn't going anywhere. Sure, eventually he would get up and begin walking home. But he wouldn't be moving forward. He was stuck, and he was going to be stuck for a very long time. Maybe forever. Stuck with the reality of what he missed, stuck with the guilt, stuck with the pain.

Stuck with the memory.

He sat there thinking about it all, the seconds passing like the shadow on a sundial. Tears were flowing, but his face and eyes were so soaked from the rain no one would have been able to tell. This provided camouflage should anyone happen by while he was sitting there. Not that anyone was out in this weather.

He was the only one crazy enough…

Suddenly a person appeared. He came up from behind Marty and stood next to the bench. Initially, Marty just kept his gaze affixed to the ground beneath his feet. But curiosity and a little fear overcame him and he turned to see a man who had come to a stop just a couple of feet to his left.

He was holding an umbrella, which veiled his face. The stranger was wearing what appeared to be a white lab coat, underneath which were a white button down shirt with a black tie and plain khaki pants. On his feet were white leather all-purpose shoes. He turned toward Marty, and as he did he raised the umbrella so that Marty could now see his features. He looked like he was probably in his late fifties or early sixties. He appeared middle-eastern. His skin was dark olive, eyes deep brown, and his nose had a small hump almost two-thirds of the way down its slope. His head was bald on the very top, hair on the back and sides. The hair was grey mixed with white, so thick it resembled a rabbit's pelt.

He began to speak to Marty as if they already knew one another, which was alarming. His voice sounded smooth, a definite accent but not nearly thick enough to make it difficult to hear what he was saying. He had to repeat what he said only because Marty wasn't paying attention to his words. He was still stunned this interaction was taking place. *Where did he come from? Why was he here? Am I in danger?*

"Why are you sad?" the stranger repeated.

"What makes you think I'm sad?" Marty responded, a little too quickly. He didn't wait for a response before he dipped his head again and continued staring at the ground, rain still streaming through his hair and on down to the sidewalk below the bench.

"Because you are sitting out in the rain. Only people in great joy or great sorrow choose to be out in the rain. You don't appear to be in great joy, if you don't mind my saying so."

"I appreciate it," Marty said sarcastically, without raising his head this time. The man was right. He thought back to a time when the rain had brought great joy into his life. He noted to himself while this stranger wasn't exactly exuding warmth, he did have a soothing presence. His demeanor was disarming, not friendly, but parental. Maybe even scholarly, like wisdom was oozing out of his pores. Still, he was a stranger, and Marty was wary of the man's intentions.

"Would you like to talk about why you're sad?" the man asked.

"I don't think that's any of your business," Marty replied. "Who are you anyway? And what are you doing here?"

"You can call me Professor," the man said, ignoring the second question.

What is this, Gilligan's Island? Marty joked to himself. "Professor, huh? What do you teach, *Professor*?" Marty asked with more than a hint of mocking. He was ready to be done with this conversation, ready for the stranger to move on.

"My field is <u>human neuropsychiatry</u>, among other things. Would you like to talk about why you're sad?" he asked again.

The Professor's question was met with silence. Marty lifted his head, but didn't look toward the man. He was hoping his silence would effectively end the conversation, hoping he could go back to being alone. The rain was still coming down fairly steady. The puddles beneath the bench growing into pools that rippled every time a new drop hit.

The Professor began moving, and Marty was relieved. *Thank God he finally took the hint.* But to his surprise and disappointment, the man took a seat on the wet bench next to Marty. *Alright, if you're not going to go away, let's hear your story, Professor.*

"So, human neuropsychology, eh? Sounds like a good time. Where do you teach?"

"Neuropsychiatry. I teach as an adjunct professor at many different colleges," the Professor answered. "Here's my card."

"Oh yeah? I'm in my fourth year at U of T. Business Management major," Marty answered, taking the card but not looking at it. He transferred it to the hand opposite the Professor and tried to nonchalantly slide it down between the opening of the wooden bench. But it got stuck on some gum and just hung there in the space between. As Marty briefly tried to stuff it further down, he picked his head back up when he realized the Professor had continued talking. The rain was making it a bit difficult to hear.

"Well, Marty, I've made it my business to know everything there is to know about the way the human brain processes information. Specifically as it relates to memory." the Professor said. "Human memory is a powerful thing. It's a fascinating field of study, really. Memory is a key to unlocking our understanding of all manner of human behavior. People are the way they are for a reason, and memory is a big part of the reason. Explore a man's memory, and you embark upon a journey of figuring out why he does what he does. It is the key to a person's happiness or bitterness or contentment or strife. Memory is everything."

"Yep, I suppose it is," Marty replied, not really paying attention.

The Professor continued, undeterred. "In fact, I'd be willing to wager you're out here in this rain because of a memory you cannot get away from. Your pain, your sorrow, your lack of concern for being uncomfortably wet, your surrendered disposition, your defeated body language. All of it due to something in your mind, something in the past, something you just can't shake. A terrible memory."

The man was slowly, steadily gaining more of Marty's attention. *Nice educated guess,* thought Marty. *Most could have come to the same conclusion given the available data.* Still, he was intrigued. Something about this stranger seemed powerful, in a way that made him a bit uncomfortable and yet drawn to him. A completely unexpected development based on his initial impression.

Up until a few moments ago all he wanted was to be left alone, for this man to go away. But now he wanted to hear a little more, even if he wouldn't have admitted it out loud. The man had taken the time to sit here, in the rain, and provide him with some company when he felt completely alone. Sure, he had an umbrella and he certainly hadn't paid much attention to Marty's attempts at making him go away, but the spot he was sitting on the bench had been soaked before he sat down, and the umbrella wasn't doing much for him at all. And maybe it was good he was doing all of the talking.

Marty didn't want to talk anyway.

"It's okay. You don't have to tell me," The Professor said after a few moments of silence. "I've been around long enough to read the signs. I believe it was Steinbeck who said, 'One can find so many pains when the rain is falling.'

"It's just that, I can't help you if you don't talk."

"Help me?" Marty said, before he thought about it. He sounded defensive and angry and he knew it. "Nobody can help me." Marty relented, his voice trailing off as he hung his head again.

"What you mean is you cannot help yourself. And it is true, you cannot. But I can."

"I don't see how." Marty said.

"It's not by chance you and I have met here this evening, nor is this rain insignificant," the Professor continued, brushing past Marty's skepticism.

"What's the rain got to do with it?"

"Clearly, you wanted to be alone. You counted on
nobody else choosing to stay out in the rain. But I am not
like anybody else. I have deep patience and understanding.
Part of you being out here with no umbrella or rain gear
was to torture yourself. You not only are in deep pain
because of some memory you cannot escape, but you are
harboring a great deal of guilt as well. You hold yourself
responsible for whatever it is you are trying to forget.
Which makes it even more difficult to put it out of your
mind. When we blame ourselves for a great tragedy, the
mind becomes our own personal agent of torture. And the
enemy of our soul whispers to us *through* our mind and
convinces us we cannot have peace, do not deserve to be
free. And so you have chosen to be out in the rain not only
to be alone, but to continue the process of punishing
yourself for your sins. If it hadn't been raining, you
wouldn't have been at this bus stop. I wouldn't have come
upon you, wouldn't have sensed your great sorrow and the
opportunity to help you.

"No, you and I meeting here in this place is no
coincidence."

"I don't know about all of that," Marty said, even
though he couldn't really argue with anything the
Professor said. He had identified, exactly, the condition of

Marty's heart. And the combination of his persistence, sincere concern, and wisdom had made Marty feel he could trust the man, even though they had just met. Anybody could have guessed he was sad, but he had really nailed the guilt and self-torture part. It was like he was reading his mind, maybe even speaking the language of his heart. The way he spoke with authority and understanding made Marty feel like he was talking with a prophet of some sort. At least the way he imagined having a conversation with a prophet might be. He remembered spiritual stories from his childhood about people having encounters with prophets, and from what he could recall, there always was a mixture of intimidation, amazement, and, ultimately, peace, accompanying those encounters. And that's exactly how it had gone so far. Except irritation and disinterest had preceded intimidation in this case. Extreme irritation and disinterest. But things had changed quickly. Now all Marty wanted was to find out if this stranger really could help him.

"Marty, there are always two ways out of every bad situation. One is more difficult at first, and leads to freedom later. One is freeing at first, and leads to more difficulty later. You must choose for yourself which path you want to go down."

"What do you mean?" Marty asked, now fully engaged. *When did I tell him my name?*

"I can only help you by offering you two choices. Two paths. Only one of which you can go down. And once you choose, there may be no turning back."

"Okay. I'll play along. What are the choices?"

"The first path is much more difficult in the short term. It will require us spending time together, talking through the events leading up to your personal loss. It will necessitate you going deep inside your pain to learn more of yourself, glean what you can from your mistakes, and, eventually gain peace and perspective. It could take years to get there."

No thank you, what else you got?

"The second path is immediate relief."

"Yeah. Right. Okay. And just how are you going to provide immediate relief?"

"I would bring you into my lab and completely erase the memory of whatever is haunting you so deeply. It will not even require you telling me the memory causing you so much pain."

"Excuse me?"

"I have been fortunate enough in my studies over the years to have made some rather remarkable discoveries, one of which is I have created a procedure to isolate, and erase, specific memories…"

"You've created what?!" Marty blurted out. "What do you mean, you can go inside someone's brain and wipe out a selected memory? Or a group of memories?"

"Well, yes, but I didn't finish…"

"What about an entire person? Can you erase the memory of an entire person from someone's mind? Like they never even existed?"

"Yes, yes I can. I don't recommend it. But it can be done."

"But how?" Marty wondered aloud. It was too good to be true.

"Well, even if I wanted to explain it to you, without an extensive knowledge of human neuropsychiatry, you won't be able to understand it."

"Have you done it before? I mean, to real people, not just in a lab?" Marty pressed, undeterred.

"Yes. On rare occasions, afflicted people have come to me for help, and I have used the power at my disposal to provide relief to those who lead tortured lives."

"Unbelievable. So what now, Professor?" Marty asked, not mocking this time.

"Now you must make a choice."

"I've already made up my mind. I cannot live like this any longer. I can't sleep, I can't eat, I can't function. And this has been going on for longer than I care to remember. Something has to change. I'll try anything."

"Have you considered the possibility of time healing these wounds?"

"Time hasn't done anything for me. In fact, time only makes it worse. Each passing day is harder than the last."

"Surely there will be a day when it turns, though."

"I don't believe it."

"You've made up your mind then?"

"If you're serious about trying to help me, I'm desperate enough to give it a shot. I'm at rock-bottom. I don't see how it can get any worse."

"Well, then, if we are going to do this, we must do it quickly. Tomorrow, if possible. There are consent forms I will need you to sign, and some other, um, requirements you will need to satisfy before we can begin the procedure."

"Well, I was just planning on sitting at this bus stop in the rain again tomorrow, but I guess I can clear up my schedule. What kind of requirements?"

"Let us get out of this rain. I see a diner on the corner across the street. There I will tell you all you need to do to prepare yourself."

Chapter Three

"I use memories, but I will not allow memories to use me." - Deepak Chopra

Marty left the hallway and entered the main room, close on the heels of the man holding the box. This area of the house was probably at one time a living room or sitting area, with a big window on one side that had been blacked out. There was a stone fireplace on the far end, a few logs crackling with fire. The room was utilitarian, out of place for a residential dwelling. No warmth, all business. It smelled like a place old people had lived in and Marty thought of his grandparents' house.

The large open area had been converted into what Marty imagined an oral surgeon's operating room would look like. Grey walls, tile floor, sparse fluorescent lighting fixtures providing dim, grey light. Along the wall opposite the window was basic cabinetry, with ample counter space and a sink in the center. The counters were covered with a few medical supplies, cotton swabs, boxes of syringes, packages of gauze, containers of latex gloves. In the center of the room was a chair. It was off-white patent leather with a thick plastic cover over the surface. It had arm rests with straps on the end and a cushioned head rest near the top. Above it was a light with handles on either side, attached to an adjustable arm.

"Put this on," the Professor said, handing Marty a generic hospital gown. "You can keep your jeans on, just remove your shirt."

Marty quickly pulled his shirt over his head and let it fall to the floor near his feet. He slid his arms through the sleeves of the gown. He tied it in the back and stood there, not bothering to do anything about his shirt on the floor.

"Be seated," the man said, as he motioned toward the chair with his right hand. With his left hand, he placed the box down on the counter closest to the fireplace. In the box was everything the Professor told him to include. *"Anything connecting you to the memory,"* he had instructed. *"Pictures, notes, gifts, jewelry, knick-knacks, whatever. Place it all in the box. All of it. Leave nothing out or it could jeopardize the entire process. Restore your cell phone to its original settings and change the number, cancel your social media accounts. Then bring the box with you to this address no more than four hours after you pack it. You need not worry whether or not I will be home. I know you will come. And I will be waiting for you."* He started packing the box right at 2 p.m. And arrived just after 5:30 p.m. Marty had done everything as he was supposed to.

This had to work.

Marty moved toward the white chair and lowered himself onto it by sitting sideways and then slowly swinging his legs up. The Professor joined him at the side of the chair. He strapped Marty's right wrist down to the arm rest, then quickly moved around to the other side of

28

the chair and repeated the same action on the left side. Marty instinctively clenched the muscles in both forearms and raised them up to test the resistance of the restraints. The muscles in Marty's stomach tightened even more and he struggled to fight the anxiety slowly metastasizing from the center of his chest up into his throat. His heart was beating fast now, so fast that he was fully aware of each pulsating pump. He struggled to swallow and breaths were becoming more and more shallow. *This is it,* he thought.

There was no turning back now.

In a strange house, with a strange man, about to undergo a procedure he knew dangerously little about. A decision he understood would alter not only the course of his future, but the way he remembered his past. It was crazy, all of it.

People do crazy things when they are imprisoned by their own grief and guilt.

"You said you were a professor. How do you know so much about medical stuff like anesthesia?" Marty was trying to reassure himself.

"I am many things. I am a professor, a philanthropist, a builder, a father, a doctor. But teaching is my passion, so I usually stick with Professor. And I never said anything about anesthesia."

"You're not going to put me under?"

"I didn't say that, either."

The Professor attached several patches to the sides of Marty's head. They were connected by wires which ran to some sort of fancy monitor behind the dentist chair. The Professor then took Marty's arm and wrapped it with a sleeve and checked his blood pressure and pulse. He then fed Marty a pill with a small sip of water. "This is the good stuff," the Professor said. "This will ease your nerves and make you feel relaxed and comfortable. I need you to listen to me very carefully…"

The Professor reiterated what he had told Marty at the diner the night before. "You don't have to tell me who you want to forget. In this procedure, what's happening in your brain is all that matters. You need to focus on the circumstances surrounding the first time you met the person you want to erase from your memory. The synapses in your brain will fire in a certain pattern when you do this. It will help me to locate the memory and re-program the nerve endings. From there, I can do what needs to be done."

Marty was superficially listening, but the talons of his mind were already reaching back to a particular day. A day which had been like any other day. Until it wasn't.

The day he met *her*.

It's funny when a generic word ends up becoming something more. When a primitive word like *her* or *him* evolves and takes on a life of its own. You don't know it when it happens, this invisible moment when a personal pronoun becomes a noun, a proper name. Like many of the best transformations in life, it happens at a level below the conscious mind. You wake up one day and things are different. And not just different in a temporary way. Different for good. An organization or team develops into a family, a job becomes a calling, a person you enjoy spending time with becomes someone you don't care to live without. It happens all the time.

For Marty, *her* was Mariana Jane Carson. And no one else.

Did he really want to forget *her*? It was *she* who made him feel alive for the very first time, *she* who showed him the world was good and what love really looks like. It was *she* who unlocked places in his heart he didn't even know existed before, *she* who encouraged and believed in his dreams, *she* who awoke his soul to the infinite beauty and goodness of life. How could he forget *her*? He had to. There was no other way to say it. He had to erase the memory of *her*. The memory of what they shared, but was no longer possible. The memory of what happened to *her,* and his responsibility for all of it.

It had become an anchor around the neck of his spirit, a weight so crushing he could sometimes barely breathe.

"Do you understand what I am saying to you?" the Professor asked, bringing Marty back into focus on the present situation. As Marty stared blankly back at him, the Professor reiterated what he had just finished saying. "It is of utmost importance you are recalling the precise moment you met. If there are any prior meetings you are unaware of, the procedure may be in danger of failing at some point. Also, anyone else who happens to be associated with the time of your first encounter may also be eliminated from your memory as well, depending on the strength of your connection." *No problem, there,* thought Marty.

The only other person in the scene would have been his cranky boss, and he would have loved to put him out of his mind for good. *No way I'm that lucky.*

"Got it," said Marty. But it wasn't a fluid or particularly strong response. A little too much tongue in the enunciation. The initial meds were kicking in. He was starting to feel free and disconnected from his surroundings. *Ah, yes. The good stuff.* Marty was still alert enough to remember a similar feeling from the tonsillectomy he went through in the eighth grade. *Better not let that memory get going. Don't want to forget my parents and sister. Well, at least not my parents.*

He saw the Professor move toward the box he had brought with him and relocate it to the mantle on top of the fireplace, reaching down to stoke the fire with a poker laying to the side of the opening. The tight feeling briefly reappeared in Marty's stomach. *This is a mistake,* it groaned. But the drugs made it easier to suppress this time.

Before he realized it, the Professor was back at his side, as if he covered the space between them with a snap of his fingers. This time, he had nothing in his hands. "I want you now to take your mind to the time you met the person you want to forget. Try to think of every detail. The weather, your mood, the sights, the sounds, the smells, what they were wearing, what you did, all of it. Let your memory be as specific as it wants to be. If all goes according to plan, when you awake it will be as if that moment never even happened. As a precaution, I will also erase the previous four hours leading up to this moment. You will remember meeting me, deciding to go through with the procedure, and everything occurring up until you began packing the box. If you were strict about the 4-hour window, you won't be able to remember packing the box or anything you placed inside it." The Professor placed his hands on either side of Marty's head near the temples and began rubbing them, slowly and firmly in a circular pattern.

Marty closed his eyes, and remembered the day he met Jane.

~~~ ~~~ ~~~ ~~~ ~~~ ~~~ ~~~

Marty had been watching the cars slosh by in the rain outside the coffee shop where he was finishing up his afternoon shift. He didn't love this job, but it was work, and it helped him pay the bills while he was finishing up his first year at the University. It also gave him an opportunity to meet a lot of interesting people. Marty loved people, loved hearing about their lives. *Everyone has a story*, he often mused to himself. His eyes caught sight of a person on a bicycle who was clearly not anticipating the rain. *Man, he must be hating life right now*, thought Marty, as his gaze followed the poor, soaked person as they sped past the shop. He was startled when the bell rang above the door as it suddenly opened right into him. In his attention to the wet cyclist, he didn't even realize he had moved right in front of the entrance of the shop to continue watching.

The door stopped abruptly as it met his black work shoes and in stumbled a woman covering her head with a copy of the town newspaper. She was startled by the sudden door stoppage and brought her makeshift head covering down to see what had caused the disruption. Marty stumbled back a bit, a little from the surprise of the moment and a little from the striking green eyes of the girl carrying the newspaper. She was soaked, and stunning. Marty smiled, apologized profusely, and then rushed behind the counter to retrieve a towel. He came back to where she was standing and extended the towel to her. She thanked him and attempted to dry the parts of her hands, arms, and face not covered by the newspaper.

"Hope you weren't planning on reading that." Marty blurted out the first thing to come to his mind, pointing to the mushy newspaper she was still holding in her right hand. *Trying to be clever, there, kid? She probably thinks you're an idiot*, he scolded himself. She cracked a slight smile - an opening perhaps? - and responded, "No, I actually don't read the paper. I only get them for the crosswords. I do them in class when I'm bored with the lecture. But I'm not very good at them at all."

"Well, then today is your lucky day," Marty said, faking confidence.

Intrigued, if only the slightest, she played along, "How so?"

"I'm pretty good at crossword puzzles." Marty said, trying to sound sure and humble at the same time.

"Pretty good?"

"Quite good."

"That's very interesting. You have a name, crossword man?"

"Marty," he responded, sticking out his hand, "Marty Drake." *Thank God she said "man" and not "boy"*.

"Well, Marty Drake, I'm not sure I'm worthy to shake hands with a crossword savant," she teased, then took his hand in hers. As she did Marty felt something move up his arm straight into his chest. *What in the world*?

"I'm Jane," she said. "Jane Carson."

"It's a pleasure to meet you," Marty said, trying to keep his composure. "My shift is over in about 10 minutes," He continued, gathering some momentum. "Why don't you sit here and dry off for a bit. Go ahead and start the puzzle, if it's still dry, and when I clock out, I'll come finish it. If I can't finish it, I owe you a coffee. If I do finish it, you go out to dinner with me this Saturday."

"I'm tempted to take you up on that bet. My wallet is empty and I'm in desperate need of a white chocolate mocha to warm me up. You do realize this is the Times and not the school newspaper, right? The Times crossword is much more difficult."

"Well, I guess we'll see in a few minutes." he said, downshifting. It was as humble a response as he could think of in the moment. It was feigned humility, and he hoped it worked. He knew he would finish it. He had to.

Marty moved to take his place back behind the counter. It was only then he noticed his manager, Joe, had been glaring at him. There was a line of four people and they were not interested in waiting out his flirtation before they received their afternoon caffeine fix. The weather certainly wasn't helping anyone's mood. Marty doubled his step, lifted the hinged counter top and took his place filling coffee orders for the final minutes of his shift. Tall Caramel Macchiato, no whip. Venti Chai Latte. Grande non-fat Hazelnut Latte. Grande Espresso Machiatto.

All the while he was keeping tabs on the new girl at her table in the corner. If she was paying any attention to him, she was doing a great job of pretending she wasn't. She seemed to be really concentrating on the puzzle, and this made him smile.

The last few minutes passed by like a cargo train moving through an intersection. As he tidied up the stations, he noticed the rain had let up a bit outside. He worried she might decide to get up and leave. He didn't have any contact info - he either wasn't brave enough or didn't have enough time to ask, he wasn't sure which. Maybe it was a little of both. He could always find her on social media, but he wasn't going to. He was a bit of an old-soul, perhaps old-fashioned. He would say it was because he was too busy to check it, but the truth was he just didn't like it.

When the clock finally moved to 5 p.m., Marty removed his apron, hung it behind the door leading to the employees only area, and paused. He needed to gather himself, plus he didn't want to appear too eager. Girls sense eagerness like dogs can sense fear. And they are repelled by it. He took a deep breath, and as he began the short walk to the corner booth where Jane was still busy working on the puzzle, he settled into his normal strut, making sure to look around the entire shop as he went. This was a strength of his, this confident walk. His closest friend had described it as "frame control" at one point. When Marty asked what he meant, his friend remarked how casual and unaffected he appeared when he was walking - totally in control. "It's all smoke and mirrors" was Marty's self-deprecating, but accurate response.

When he reached the table where Ms. Carson was sitting, she didn't lift her eyes. She was busy filling in an answer to the puzzle, with a look of focused determination on her face and the tip of her tongue poking out slightly from the corner of her mouth. From his vantage point, Marty could tell she still had a ways to go. *Yes!* was his initial thought. *Calm yourself, cowboy,* he chastised himself immediately after. He stood there for a moment, alternating between watching her work and pretending to check his cell phone. He was hoping she would break the silence, but she didn't. Of course she didn't. These things were never easy. And maybe they shouldn't be. The distraction of his cell phone gave him a brief opportunity to think about how he would continue the conversation, and in a few seconds he had a fierce argument in his head with at least five competing and equally terrible openers.

He decided to go with simple.

"How are you making it, there?"

"Oh, about like usual. I get the easy ones and I know most of the clues common to all puzzles. It's the more obscure references I have trouble with."

Marty blurted, "Well, 'obscure' is my middle name," and immediately regretted it. He had been doing so well! He felt his face flush and his body temperature began to creep up. Moisture was forming under his armpits.

"Marty Obscure Drake?"

She was being playful. Thank goodness. *Be cool.*

"Weird, right? My parents were hippies." she laughed. Apparently a genuine laugh.

Saved, for the moment.

"You ready to surrender and give me a crack at finishing it?"

"Give me one more minute, the answer to this clue is on the tip of my tongue."

"Yeah, I can see that," Marty said, as Jane became conscious about her tongue, that was again poking out of the side of her mouth. She quickly retracted it back into her mouth, and blushed a little.

God, she's adorable.

Marty smiled, pulled out the chair across from her, and sat down. Leaning forward in the metal chair and crossing his arms for support. He watched her fill in another blank and he noticed the tip of Jane's tongue involuntarily make its appearance again in the corner of her mouth and he thought about how nice it would be to kiss her right there in that spot.

"Ok, I give up," she said, startling him back into reality. She slowly pushed the paper toward him in surrender. He grabbed it and spun it around in front of him. And as she handed him the pencil their hands touched and he had the same sensation he felt earlier when they shook hands for the first time. *Focus*, he reminded himself. *It's time to win a date with Jane Carson.*

There were about twenty unanswered clues in the puzzle, and he could have finished it in less than three minutes. But he wanted to drag this initial encounter out as long as possible. He paused a few seconds between figuring out each clue and filling in the answer. Just over seven minutes had passed by the time he filled in the answer to the last clue, "Launch." He filled in the I and the T of the answer, "initiate", and set the pencil down on the table.

"What time should I pick you up on Saturday?" he asked.

"How do I know you actually filled in the correct answers?" she shot back. "You could have filled in random letters."

"Check for yourself," Marty said, spinning the paper back in front of her. She studied it for a few seconds and then looked up at him, with a coy expression.

"What time? Seven p.m.?" Marty repeated.

"Seven it is, Marty Drake. Call me tomorrow at this number and we'll talk about the details," she said writing her number on a napkin and then pushing it across the table to him.

"You got it."

"I've got to get going. Night class." She said, and rose from the table. "I never did get a white chocolate mocha. Thanks for nothing."

"This is true, but I'm really glad we ran into each other. Well, technically, you ran into me."

"Only because you were standing in the middle of the doorway." she answered.

"Good point. Well, I guess I'll talk to you tomorrow. Have a good night."

"You, too." Said Jane, finishing the conversation. She picked up the paper from the table and dropped it in the trash can on the way out the door. Marty was right behind her, and as he headed to his bike, he stopped himself. Making sure she was out of sight, he jogged back inside the coffee shop. He reached down into the trash can, pulled out the paper with the completed crossword puzzle, rolled it up and stuck it under his arm. When he looked up, Joe was looking at him with a disapproving scowl on his face. Marty just smiled, shrugged, and headed back out the door.

~~~ ~~~ ~~~ ~~~ ~~~ ~~~ ~~~

He had clipped the crossword puzzle out and put it away in a box. Later, he would have it laminated and framed as a gift to her on the anniversary of their first date. He wasn't sure why he had retrieved it out of the trash other than a hunch this might be something special. Or maybe it was blind hope. He tried to remember what it was like, having blind hope. Or any kind of hope at all. It was hanging out there somewhere in the murkiness of his heart, but it floated on a string in the ever-narrowing bright part of his soul, just out of reach.

The laminated crossword puzzle was only a few feet away from him now, in a file box, sealed with red duct tape, with the word JANE written in black permanent marker across the side. Along with pictures, notes, a lottery ticket, a birthday card, a CD with her favorite song, a rolled up piece of art she had created, and many more ordinary, priceless things. With groggy eyes, he noticed the

Professor, who was now more like a shadow, move toward the box and pick it up. He walked over to the fire and situated the box over the burning logs.

The last thing Marty saw before he drifted into another world was the flames ferociously and methodically licking their way up the side of the box.

Chapter Four

"How can we live without our lives? How will we know it's us without our past?" - John Steinbeck

When Marty regained consciousness, his mind powered up slowly, like a dormant computer screen warming up. His senses were returning one by one. He could feel a slight breeze move across his face as the sounds of a few passing cars made their way to his ears and the aroma of outdoors crept its way into his nostrils. He slowly smacked his lips together a few times, while his brain tried to process all of the data it was receiving. He was outside, for sure. But why?

His eyes opened with a start and he quickly sat up.

His right hand moved to rub his eyes and also to shield them from the bright sun and its rude invasion, while his left hand helped to provide stability for his awakening body. He was woozy and his head was pounding. As his eyes adjusted to the sunlight, he started to get his bearings. He was on the same bus stop bench he had been on when he met the Professor the day before. Or was it two days ago? What day was it? Why was he back here? He sat there for a while, maybe a long while, and tried to recall the events leading up to where he was right now.

He couldn't remember a thing since around lunchtime the day before. He had made himself a sandwich and ate it while watching an episode of a popular sitcom on television at his apartment.

His apartment. That's where he needed to get to. He needed to take a painkiller for this headache, needed to lay down, recharge, regroup. He slowly rose from the bench and took a moment to get his balance, like a patient getting up from a hospital bed after surgery. He noticed, for the first time, he was wearing a hospital gown to go along with his favorite pair of jeans, and an old pair of running shoes. He had no shirt on underneath the gown and the wind was blowing up through it. It felt good, but he was embarrassed and didn't want anyone to see him dressed like this. He looked around, self-conscious, hoping nobody was paying attention to him.

Dammit. He made eye-contact with a man across the street and to his right. The stranger was leaning against the hood of an orange VW Bug. In one hand, he was holding a half-eaten apple, and in the other, what appeared to be a book. As their eyes met, he took another bite of his apple and went back to reading. There was something about the man that made Marty uneasy. He was maybe in his early 30's, with an impressive-looking beard, wearing a plaid shirt, faded blue jeans, and work boots. He looked as if he was trying to act like he wasn't interested in Marty's presence, even though he really was. *Has he been watching me?* Marty quickly dismissed the thought and tried to shake off the uneasiness he felt.

He pushed the gown down and tucked it into his jeans and turned left down the sidewalk headed to his apartment, casually glancing over his right shoulder to make sure he wasn't being followed. The bearded man was still leaning up against the car, apparently reading his book.

Marty tried to walk fast, even considered jogging at one point, but his head and legs were in no shape to withstand the demands of athletic activity. It took about twenty minutes before he reached the parking lot of his complex. He cut across the main lot and located his building, number five. As he started toward the stairs, out of the corner of his eye he saw a flash of orange and turned to see what he thought was the tail end of a 60's model car before it disappeared slowly on the other side of building four. "What the…" Marty mumbled under his breath. He wondered if it was the same car he had seen, if the same strange, bearded man was behind the wheel. And if either or both of those were true, what did it mean? It was probably just a coincidence, but he couldn't shake the growing paranoia he felt.

He changed direction and headed off to investigate. Marty moved as quickly as his swimming head and wobbly legs would allow; his temples were pounding and nausea was settling in over his stomach. When he got to the corner near the parking lot where he had seen the car, he slowed down. He crept up to the building and pressed his back to it, scooting the last few feet like he had seen people do in the movies. *How many of our actions are based on what we've seen in movies?* He thought to himself and felt silly. Nevertheless, the things he'd experienced in the last twenty-four hours would certainly make for a good movie, and he was a bit spooked by the idea of someone potentially following him, so he stuck with his approach.

At the corner there was a tree which provided cover for him to observe the parking lot next to apartment building four. He situated himself between the tree and the wall and began looking over the cars in the lot. It was midday, so the lot was mostly empty, with only about fifteen cars spread out over seventy available spaces. Orange! He spotted a small orange vehicle diagonally behind an off-white SUV about thirty feet to his left. It only took him a few seconds of focus and standing on his tip-toes to determine it was just an old hatchback - not the same car. He realized his heart rate had skyrocketed at the sight of the color and he could feel his pulse thumping in his temples.

As his eyes moved from car to car, he began to feel a sense of relief. *I've got to sleep off this hangover*, Marty thought and turned to walk back to his apartment.

"HEY!"

Marty heard an accusing shout from a man who was approaching him and only a few feet away. By the time it registered what was happening, the man was right up in his face.

"What do you think you're doing?" he demanded.

Marty said nothing.

"That's my girlfriend's apartment right there, creep."

Marty looked to where the man was pointing and for the first time noticed the window near the tree he had been hiding behind. *Crap.* Marty considered telling the truth, then he considered lying. In the end, he settled for something in the middle.

"I'm so sorry. It's not what you think. I had a medical procedure yesterday, and I'm a little disoriented from the medication. When I got home, I took my dog for a walk and he got away. I was trying to find him. I apologize if I alarmed you in any way."

The man, not buying this half-truth, continued to stand in front of Marty, arms-crossed, jaw set, his body language indicating he wasn't going to move until Marty left. Marty nodded, walked past him and began calling out, "Dizzy!

Here, Dizzy! Come on, boy. Dizzzzy!" until he was out of earshot of the man, who watched Marty for a minute before disappearing into his girlfriend's apartment.

When Marty reached the stairs of building five once again, he summoned the last bit of energy he had remaining to scale the three floors to get to his apartment. He walked to the door of his unit, took the key out of his pocket, unlocked the deadbolt, and then the door knob. Walking inside, the familiar smell of home eased him a bit and he walked to his bedroom. Too exhausted and in too much pain to worry about anything any longer, he collapsed on the bed, not even bothering to get under the covers.

In a matter of moments, he was asleep again.

Outside Marty's apartment, a bearded man wearing a flannel shirt, faded blue jeans, and work boots whispered "528" to himself as he wrote the number down in the top corner of his dog-eared book. He put the pen back in his shirt pocket and stuffed the book behind his back between his jeans and his shirt. He then turned and walked casually back toward the stairs and descended back to the parking lot.

Chapter Five

"If you're going to steal, steal a heart.." - Hitch

"Well hey there, stranger!"

It was Marty's sister, Mel, greeting him at the front door of her house. They hadn't seen each other in months. Marty was terrible at keeping in touch, and they both knew it, but with everything Marty had experienced in the last 24 hours, he needed the comfort of familiar faces. So he called her up and asked if they could meet for dinner. He meant for them to meet out somewhere, but Mel had hospitality in her bones, and she insisted they meet at her house.

"Hey Mel, it's good to see you," Marty said, leaning in for a hug.

"Come on in! Oh, and I'm sorry for the mess. I didn't have much time to get everything together."

What mess? This place is immaculate as always. Why are women always apologizing for messes that don't exist?

"The place looks great, Mel."

"David is out on the back porch, finishing up the steaks," she responded, ignoring Marty's compliment. "Dinner should be ready in just a few minutes. Have a seat and catch me up on your life."

Not a chance of that.

"Oh, you know. Just work and school. Nothing out of the ordinary." Marty said. It was the first time he could ever remember lying to his sister. He had always been able to tell her anything. Four years older, she had always been there, a second mom in the best possible sense, always looking out for him, always available to talk about anything. But he had no idea how he would even begin to talk about what he was going through now. It was too soon. Eventually, he was sure he would bring her in the loop, but at the moment he just wanted to put it out of his mind.

"What's been going on with you?"

Mel told Marty of their beach vacation, her frustrations with work, and her and her husband David's continued attempts to get pregnant, which so far were yielding no results.

"I'm sorry, sis."

"Thank you. It's ok. It will happen when it's supposed to happen, and not a moment before."

Mel always had a way of looking at the bright side of any situation. Marty had always admired her for that.

After a few minutes, David came in with the steaks. Marty greeted him, helped Mel finish setting the table, and the three of them sat down to eat. They drank red wine and laughed about old times. David told a funny story of something he experienced at work the day before, and Mel made sure everyone's glass never ran dry.

After dinner, they moved to the living room. Mel got out some photos albums and they flipped through them.

They both laughed at a photo of Marty around four years old. He was wearing shorts, a sweater, and a plastic football helmet, a football resting between his legs.

"This was right around the time of the 'washing machine incident.'" Mel said, giggling as she spoke.

Marty had no idea what she was talking about.

"What's the 'washing machine incident'?"

"Oh stop playing dumb. You know exactly what I'm talking about, silly. It may be an embarrassing moment for you, but you can't deny it happened."

"Deny *what* happened? I honestly don't remember."

Mel thought Marty was messing with her because it was something they brought up with each other and laughed about frequently. And Marty thought Mel was messing with him, because he really had no idea what she was referring to. The story of Marty wetting the bed as a four-year-old and then attempting to wash the sheets before their mom found out. He got a chair to climb up to the washing machine, somehow figured out how to turn it on, and, as he was pouring detergent into the basket, it slipped out of his hand and the whole container emptied into the washing machine. Panicked, he quickly shut the lid, climbed down from the chair, left the laundry room, and went to hide in his room. It was about fifteen minutes later their mother came in to the laundry room and found the washing machine overflowing with suds.

"What do you mean you don't remember?" Mel said. "Stop playing around. We've joked about this just about every time we've been together for the last fifteen years." Marty, trying to mask his confusion and slight panic, lied to his sister, again, and said he was just kidding.

"Of course I remember. How could I forget?" He said, faking a laugh. *Yes, how could you forget?*

On the outside, Marty remained calm, but on the inside a cold wave began to slowly creep over his body, like a person in class realizing they've missed an assignment due, or a driver seeing a cop in their rearview mirror when they know they've been speeding. Perhaps his recklessness was catching up with him sooner rather than later.

"You ok?" Mel asked him.

"Not really. I think I drank too much wine." It was the truth, if not the whole truth and nothing but the truth.

"You should stay the night then. No need to go home. You can sleep in here on the sofa or on the back porch like you normally do." There was an extremely comfortable old couch that used to be in the living room of their childhood home on Mel and David's screened-in back porch. Marty had slept there more than once after similar nights of catching up, eating dinner, and drinking red wine.

"Yeah I think I'll sleep out on the porch if you don't mind."

"Don't mind at all, Buddy."

Buddy is what Mel had called Marty for as long as he could remember.

"I think I'll go ahead and lay down."

It was a cool evening, and Mel made sure Marty was covered with a blanket and had a pillow before she turned out the porch light.

"If you need anything, let me know," she said, leaning down to kiss him on the forehead.

"I'm glad you came over. Get some rest, ok?"

"Ok."

"Love you, Buddy. Good night."

"Love you. Night, sis."

When he left the next morning, Marty fretted about the previous evening's forgetfulness on his bike ride home and tried to recall as many things from his childhood as he could. He couldn't be positive, but there seemed to be some definite gaps forming in his long-term memory.

Marty parked his bike on the curb next to a rack and secured it with a lock. He took off in the direction of the massive university library dominating the other buildings near the middle of the campus. It had been two days since he slept over at his sister's house.

He was looking for something, anything able to explain what had been happening to him since he allowed the man who called himself the Professor to erase a part of his memory. He was only supposed to get rid of one memory - a person, maybe? - he remembered that much. For now, at least. With each passing day, he noticed he was forgetting more and more things.

He was fighting to keep the light panic from blooming into full-blown anxiety, but his efforts were proving mostly unsuccessful. How far would this go? Had he incurred some sort of brain damage? Was there anything he could do to stem the tide washing away the contents of his memory? These were the questions driving him to seek out answers at the school library.

He could see it up ahead. Thick, white columns out front resting on brick stairs leading up to massive wooden doors. *Maybe there are some answers in there*, Marty thought, not really believing it was true. As he was approaching the intersection before the library, he passed the on-campus coffee shop - part of the same franchise as the one he worked at a few city blocks away. He looked in the windows as he passed by, just to see if he knew anyone inside.

He slowed when he got to the corner and stopped to wait for the signal to cross the street. He had so much nervous energy he couldn't stand still. He circled around as he waited and saw a male college student emerge from the coffee shop with a sleeve-wrapped cup in his hand. The man walked over to his bike, set the coffee on the ground next to it and began to undo his bike chain, leaving the coffee unattended for a few seconds. Marty's eyes were focused in on the coffee. He had a sudden urge to walk over and take it and just keep walking.

~~~ ~~~ ~~~ ~~~ ~~~ ~~~ ~~~

**"I could really go for a cup of coffee about now."
Marty had said, off-handedly, as he and Jane made
their way through town headed towards the campus
library to study together. This was the fourth time they
had seen each other since their chance meeting at the
coffee shop. Things were progressing slowly, but
steadily. A study date seemed a good, safe, idea for
their next encounter. They had met each other at the
Quad in the middle of campus and began the walk
toward the library when Marty's coffee craving hit.**

"Well, why don't you get you one?" Jane said.

"I don't have any cash on me."

"Figures."

"What's that supposed to mean?"

"You boys and your lack of cash. I think it's a conscious or sub-conscious way of shirking your chivalric duty to pay for things."

Marty laughed, picking up on her playful tone. "Well, I don't know who you've been hanging around, but I can chival like you wouldn't believe."

"Oh really?"

"Yes ma'am. Except for right now. In this moment, I need you to buy me a cup of coffee. Then for all the rest of the times moving forward I've got you covered."

"The rest of the times? You haven't been guaranteed any more times, Mister."

"Guarantees are for wimps. I don't need any assurances. I'm confident. I'll take my chances."

"I see. Well how much of a chance are you willing to take to get some coffee?"

"I take it this means you're not going to buy me a cup?"

"Buying a cup is too easy. Let's just grab someone else's."

Marty laughed until he looked over and realized she wasn't joking.

"You're serious?"

"Completely."

"What are you, a thief?"

"Nope. I've never stolen anything, well anything but coffee."

"You're just testing me, right? Trying to figure out if I'll be the kind of person who stands up for what is right. Who is not so concerned about impressing you as to put aside basic morals and human decency."

"Absolutely not. I'll prove it to you. Just watch."

Without hesitation, Jane walked over to the corner by the on-campus coffee shop situated across from the library. There were cars moving down the street, people on bikes and on foot going back and forth between classes and lunch, and nobody was paying attention to anyone else. Except Marty. He was paying attention to the beautiful, perhaps crazy, girl acting casual outside a coffee shop. As he watched from about twenty yards away, Jane followed behind a girl who had just exited the coffee shop. The girl went to her bike, set the coffee on the ground next to it, and went to unlock her bike from the stand. As her attention was away from the cup for just a few seconds, Jane strolled by and in one continuous, fluid motion swooped down, picked up the coffee and kept walking in the opposite direction. Swept away in a sea of other people, many of whom also had cups of coffee in their hand. When the girl looked back down to pick up her coffee, she was momentarily confused. She looked around to see if she had put it in a different place. Then she checked the curb to see if it had been knocked off onto the road. When it finally dawned on her what probably happened, Jane was out of sight. The girl cursed under her breath, re-locked her bicycle to the stand, and went back into the coffee shop.

A few moments later, Marty felt a tap on his shoulder. He turned around to see a victorious Jane smiling and extending the cup of coffee to him, as if it were a gift she had purchased just for him. "Here ya go, sir. One cup of coffee, just as you requested."

"Why, you little criminal!" was what came out of Marty's mouth.

"I prefer coffee swiper."

Marty had so many things going through his mind, he didn't know where to begin. He was equal parts stunned and intrigued. "Do you do this often?"

"Only when I don't have money for coffee. And I always make up for it later."

"How? You don't ever see those people again."

"I know. But I'll pay for someone's coffee in the drive-thru or in line behind me. It's not *the* person, but it's *a* person. Close enough."

"I don't even know what to say about this." Marty said. But it wasn't judgment, or anger, or disappointment. It was...wonder.

"Well are you going to drink it before it gets cold, or not?"

"How do I know she didn't drink from it before she set it down? Maybe she's sick or a strep-carrier or something. Her germs could be all over the lid. Her backwash could be swirling around inside."

"Mister-Chivalrous-Knight-in-Shining-Armor afraid of a few little germs?" She teased.

I better drink this, thought Marty. *She did go through an awful lot to get it for me.* He found it so bewildering, this crazy act he just witnessed. It was clear she didn't care what he thought about her. She wasn't putting on to impress him. She wasn't worried about anything other than being herself. He wasn't sure what to say or do next, but he was sure he had never met anyone like Jane Carson in his whole life. Beautiful, unpredictable, funny, wild, mysterious, swiper of coffee. He put the coffee up to his lips and took a sip.

"Well?" She asked.

"It's good. Thank you very much for getting this for me. I'll never forget it."

"Good, because you're going to be the one to pay for a stranger's coffee next time," she said. Then she turned on her heels and began heading in the direction of the library again.

Marty laughed, shook his head, took another sip of the coffee and started following after her. As they passed the coffee shop, he swooped down and picked up a cup of coffee left on the ground by another distracted

biker un-locking his bike. *Yes!* **He increased his pace, came up beside Jane and held out the newly acquired coffee. She looked at him with a mix of surprise and admiration and took the cup from him.**

"Why, you little criminal," was all she said before she took a big sip.

~~~ ~~~ ~~~ ~~~ ~~~ ~~~ ~~~

Marty watched the man whose coffee he wanted to take get on his bike and start pedaling away from the library, one hand on the handlebars and the other holding the coffee. *What a strange sensation. I've never stolen anything in my life. Deja Vu, maybe?* The crosswalk light turned in his favor and he crossed the street, continuing to wonder about what he had just experienced. He headed up the stairs to the main doors of the library.

Inside the library, Marty went directly to the nearest computer and typed in the phrase 'memory loss'. Immediately, hundreds of results began to appear on the screen. Books, articles, medical journals, newspaper stories, it was overwhelming. *Looks like I've come to the right place.* He scanned the choices, paralyzed by the sheer volume of works. How would he ever choose one? The first book listed was a work entitled, *A Quest for Memory.* He was certainly on a quest for memory. *Maybe this will work.* After reading a brief description of the contents of the book, he decided it was close enough.

He jotted down the location of the book on one of the pieces of paper stacked on the desk, and headed off in the direction of the numbers on the page. He reached the proper section and began slowly moving up and down the aisles, narrowing his search. He heard the crunch of an apple being bitten into and the squeak of shoes on the hard floor the next aisle over, moving slowly. For a second it seemed if they were moving in cadence with his own. *Don't be silly*, he tried to reassure himself. When he was getting close, he began running his fingers along the books right over the numbers until the tip of his finger finally rested on the object of his search. There it was. *A Quest for Memory.* He exhaled dramatically and the tension in his shoulders released. *Please, please be helpful.* His hand moved to the top of the book and grabbed it.

He pulled it toward him and, in the opening, a pair of eyes were staring right at him.

His chest tightened just below the sternum, and he instinctively let out a yell that sounded a lot louder bouncing off the quiet walls of the library than it should have. He jumped back, strange eyes still focused on him, and his brain went into fight or flight mode. In just a few seconds, he determined the face was familiar, but not friendly. *I'm in danger.* Instinctively, he tucked the book in his back pocket and began walking briskly away.

He didn't escape to the front of the library, but to the first red EXIT sign he saw. He leaned on the crash bar and spilled through the door into a back staircase typically used for emergencies only. It was quiet. Deserted. Without looking back to see if he was being followed, he began running down the stairs, taking several at a time and he was at the ground level in a matter of moments. He burst out the back door into the bright sunlight and squinted for a moment. He oriented himself and began heading back to the front of the library. When he rounded the corner, he glanced up to the stop of the stairs and saw the man exiting the library calmly and in no hurry. They made eye contact again. And Marty began running to the spot he had parked his bike. As he was in motion, it dawned on him. The man was wearing a flannel shirt, blue jeans, and work boots. He had a thick beard. It was the same man he had seen leaning up against the orange car the day after the procedure.

The thought sent chills up his body as he slowed his jog, reached his bike, and bent down to unlock it from the stand. He hopped on, looked all around, and pedaled away. As he rode off in the opposite direction of the campus library, one jarring, unsettling, confusing reality was clear.

There was no denying it. He was being followed.

Remember Jane

Chapter Six

"No one can possibly know what is about to happen: it is happening, each time, for the first time, for the only time." - James Baldwin

Marty was asleep, his head beneath the pillow, mouth open, drool forming on the corner of his lips, one arm behind his back and the other underneath him when the sound of a ringing phone woke him with a start. "Hello?" he tried to sound like he hadn't been asleep.

Didn't work.

It was Joe. He was late for his shift at the coffee shop. "I'm so sorry. I've been studying and lost track of time." Marty lied. The truth is he hadn't planned on sleeping nearly so long. Joe mumbled something sarcastically and told Marty he better be there as soon as possible. Marty said "yes sir," and punched the red end button and took note of the time. 4:22 p.m. According to Joe, he was due at work 22 minutes ago. Realistically, he wouldn't be able to get there before 4:45 p.m., even if he skipped a shower, which he had no intention of doing.

Marty dragged himself out of bed and realized he was wearing the clothes he had on when he got back to his apartment early that morning. *These clothes stink*, he thought, as he smacked his lips together and rubbed his eyes. He quickly undressed, jumped in the shower, and tried to get his bearings. He had been staying out late at night, falling asleep on the couches of classmates after studying or partying. He would get someone to pick him up near the roundabout in the middle of the busy campus after his shifts in the evening, and then take a taxi home in the morning daylight hours.

He was grateful it was a part of college student culture to fall asleep wherever you were. In truth, he hadn't participated very often in this type of behavior, but he was adaptable. And he couldn't bear the thought of trying to sleep at home, laying awake all night wondering if and when the bearded man would try to get to him again. Hopping from couch to couch seemed much safer for the time being.

The previous night had been one of the more wilder evenings he had experienced. Marty usually didn't abuse alcohol, but the stress of his current situation got the better of him. He woke up around 7:30 a.m. on a co-worker's futon, with a thin blanket and a splitting headache both draped over him. Without waking anyone, he called a cab to take him back to his apartment. He actually couldn't recall the trek from the backseat of the cab to his bed. But clearly it had happened, somehow.

Marty was dressed in his work clothes and out the door less than fifteen minutes after Joe's wake-up call. He sprinted down the steps, unlocked his bike, and began pedaling toward the coffee shop. If he caught the lights right, he could be there in ten minutes.

He jinxed himself.

About a mile and a half from the coffee shop, the tube on the back tire on Marty's bike gave and began to feel differently underneath him. He removed his head phones and heard a dreaded, but familiar, thumping sound beneath him. He looked down, confirming what he already knew.

His back tire was flat.

You've got to be kidding me. He slowed, turned right to pop up onto a sidewalk, and brought the bike to a stop in front of a hardware store. With no options, he sent Joe a text message saying he would be even later than he thought and squatted down to lock his bike to one of the posts lining the road outside a hardware store. While still squatting, to his left his eyes settled upon a blood-draining sight. It was the orange car. He quickly clicked the lock in place and stood up. But as soon as he turned to walk down the sidewalk, he froze.

The bearded man was standing in his path.

Marty took off running in the opposite direction. Away from the coffee shop. Away from his only means of transportation. Away from anyone he actually knew. *Away from the more densely populated areas*, he noted to himself. *I'm not very bright.* He was in pretty good shape normally, but with the procedure, the chaos and confusion that followed, and the lingering grip of a hangover, he wasn't going to be able to go very long without catching his breath.

He glanced over his shoulder, hoping the man had chosen not to follow. But not only was he chasing Marty, he was gaining. *What is happening?* Marty asked himself. *What is this guy's deal?* As much as he didn't like it, there was only one way to find out. He could keep running, but the man was clearly onto his routine and knew the usual ways and arteries through which he traveled. If he wanted to get to him, to harm him, he could have easily done it already. Still, he was a strange man tracking Marty's every move. It was unsettling at best, life-threatening at worst.

But then again, things are rarely what they appear to be, are they?

It was time to make a decision. He was running out of breath, so it was either time to zig-zag his way around town, hoping he could lose the guy or he could summon some courage and confront him, letting the chips fall where they may. *I'm tired of running.* And there, in a split second, Marty made his decision. He stopped abruptly, turned around, and began walking toward the stranger, who was startled and slowed down to a walk when he saw Marty make his move. Only about fifty yards separated the two men and the closer they got to each other, the slower they walked.

When they were within about forty feet of each other, Marty suddenly stopped. This was close enough for his liking. The man, taking his cue from Marty, stopped walking after taking a few more steps. There was now about only about twenty feet between them. *What am I doing? This is trouble.* Marty thought, but he said nothing. And neither did the other man. They just stood there for a few moments, like gunslingers in the Wild West, getting ready for a draw on a hot and dusty street.

Suddenly, the stranger reached into his back pocket. Marty braced himself for the brandishing of some sort of weapon. The man slowly pulled his hands out from behind his back and as he was doing it, Marty panicked and began to walk away swiftly. *This was a mistake.* The man followed after him and when he got just behind him he began to speak. "Hey! I need to talk to you," he called ahead. But Marty didn't look back. He just picked up the pace. "I've been trying to catch up to you for a few days now." No break in Marty's gait. *I know, you've been stalking me like a psychopath.* "I can help you," the man said, now breathing a little heavier. Marty broke into a slight jog, finally gaining some separation. Then, the man stopped chasing. He just called out and said,

"I know you've seen the Professor!"

Marty stopped dead in his tracks, looked back over his shoulder in shock, and wheeled around to face the stranger. He began to march back in his direction.

"What did you say?" Marty asked, with a mix of surprise and anger, as he drew within a safe distance of the man.

"I know you've seen the Professor."

Chapter Seven

"Let's not be afraid to receive each day's surprise,
whether it comes to us as sorrow or as joy, it will open
a new place in our hearts, a place where we can
welcome new friends and celebrate more fully our
shared humanity." - Henri Nouwen

A curious, yet wary Marty just stared at the figure in front of him. *Someone else knows the Professor.* And a small pinpoint of hope pricked the dark pessimism overtaking his heart. *Maybe he can help me find him.* They just stood there, facing each other for a couple of minutes in silence. Neither one knowing quite what to do or say next.

"I'm Benjamin Pierce. You can call me Ben."

No response.

"Look, I know this has got to be unnerving at the very least. I know you're overwhelmed with all that has happened to you over the last few days, and now there's a stranger who's been following you and claims to have knowledge about what you've experienced. I know it sounds…crazy."

Crazy, bizarre, unreal, impossible.

"Believe it or not, you're not the only one who has submitted yourself to the Professor's memory-erasing procedure."

Marty looked at him intently, finally speaking. "I'm listening."

As they began walking back in the direction of where Marty parked his bike, Ben began to explain himself.

"Less than six months ago I went through the exact same thing."

"What do you mean?"

"I mean, I was in a situation where I needed to forget someone or something. I'm guessing the same was true for you. Through what seemed like happenstance at the time, I ran into the Professor. And in the most tragic decision I've ever made, I chose, as you have, to allow him to erase a part of my memory. A choice which is still rippling with life-altering consequences to this day, some of which I would like to help you avoid if at all possible. And I believe if we act quickly and prudently, we might be able to do just that."

For the first time, Marty noticed he was holding the same dog-eared book he had in his hands the day he saw him for the first time. *He really loves that book, apparently.*

When Ben noticed Marty looking at it, he admitted, "This is the journal I had in my hands the day you woke up on the bench and saw me leaning up against a car on the other side of the street. It's a diary of sorts. I've recorded most of what I've experienced over the last few months, the things I've learned, the things I've forgotten, beginning with the first few days following my procedure. They are all written down in here. I carry it with me wherever I go. After my encounter with the Professor, when I first starting noticing my memory was slipping, I went and bought the first book I could find dealing with the subject of memory. I read it, over and over again. Maybe fifteen times or more. Studying it. Memorizing it. Trying to understand it. Took pages and pages of notes in this journal. Looking for any key or edge I could find to help reverse the process. Once I felt I had a grasp on what was happening to me, I started implementing the tricks the book taught."

"Did any of them work?" Marty asked, genuinely curious.

"Some of them proved somewhat helpful to a degree, but nothing was successful in reversing it or even stemming the tide of lost memory."

"What were the ones you found helpful?"

"We may get to it later, but first you need to understand why this is happening."

"Alright," said Marty, resigned to his position of powerlessness. "Enlighten me."

As they walked, Ben nodded in the direction of a small bistro with outdoor seating. They both sat down at one of the outside tables and a server was quickly by their side, placing drink napkins and glasses of water in front of them.

"Thank you," Marty said to the server, and he was quickly gone again.

"Ok. Go." He prompted Ben.

"Ok, I'm going to do my best to explain what is going on in your brain. Keep in mind it took me a lot of studying to understand this myself, and I'm not a teacher."

"What *are* you?" Marty interrupted, curious.

"I'm a contractor. At least I was. I've forgotten all of the things I knew about my trade. I didn't recognize my workers, couldn't even place the name of some of the tools I was supposed to be using. I had to abandon a company I apparently spent years building. That's what my journal tells me, anyway. It's all disappeared from my brain. The only connection I have to my past, recent or otherwise, is what I wrote down in these pages." Ben stared off into the distance, the thought of him losing everything re-gripped his heart momentarily. He snapped back to the present moment. "Anyway, let's start with the basics. We need to talk about memory and how it works. I'm sure the Professor explained a little of the science to you, as he did me. Is this correct?"

"Yes."

"Good. It was that little bit of knowledge I used to build a theory about how he did what he did, and why it ended up causing the sweeping damage it caused. Do you have something to write with?"

"No. Why?"

"Because you should probably take notes. Your memory is in constant flux right now. There's no guarantee you'll remember any of this. If something should happen to me, or if we lose touch for any reason, I don't want you to be lost."

Marty grabbed a napkin and waved the server down to ask if he could borrow a pen. "Ok. I'm ready," he said with an attempt at a grin. "Nope, you're going to need more than that," Ben said, leaning forward to reach into his back pocket. With no fanfare, he revealed a brand new journal, identical to his own except for the color. It was red.

"This is your new best friend."

Not sure I can handle two new best friends in one day, thought Marty.

"You're going to need to become meticulous in your ability to journal, to record things you discover, things you feel, things happening to you in the present and that have happened to you in the past. Write it all down. Starting with what I'm about to share with you about my research."

"Okay. Umm, thanks for this, I guess." Marty said, motioning to the journal.

"You're welcome. You ready to go?"

"Ready or not, here we are. Let's hear what you've got."

"To put it as plainly as possible, there are a few different 'systems' in the brain working together to take input and convert it to memory. In a perfect situation, they all work together to make sure what needs to be remembered is retained and what is less important gets discarded. The main systems involved are called the frontal cortex and the hippocampus, spelled just like it sounds. They analyze the data they receive and decide what gets to stay for the long term and what goes. Initially, input is stored in short-term memory. Short-term memory is just a holding tank of sorts. It can hold up to seven items for only twenty to thirty seconds. Then the hippocampus gets involved.

"If you can imagine your brain as a library, instead of books it is filled with memories. The Hippocampus plays the role of librarian, deciding what memories to file away and which ones get sent to the trash bin. Make sense?"

"Yes, so far."

"Good, so that's just a general review of the systems and structures that help our brain retain memories. How those systems actually work with each other is a bit more complicated, but it's a clue to how the Professor was able to target and neutralize particular memories. And it's the secret to understanding why all of our other memories begin to unravel as a result."

"Ok. Let's hear it."

"Memory is all about electricity and chemicals. When the hippocampus decides to keep a memory, chemicals and electricity are the means it uses to save the data. When a memory passes from short-term to long-term memory, it has to be encoded in the language of electricity and chemicals before it gets stored. It's all about..." Ben waited for Marty to respond.

"Electricity and chemicals."

"Exactly. Every memory we have is a result of our brain re-wiring itself in order to preserve an experience we've had. Electrical impulses in the brain release chemicals called neurotransmitters. These chemicals cross the gap between the cells and form connections with each other. Those connections are called synapses. Your brain contains as many as one trillion of these suckers. And it's at these points, the synapses, where all of the good stuff happens. These connections are constantly changing. As we experience new things or, say, learn something in a classroom, more electrical impulses fire. This sends more chemicals across the gap between cells, creating new connections. Our brains are actually physically changing all the time. Tap your finger on the table."

"What? Why?"

"Just do it."

Marty began tapping his right index finger on the table.

"Just a simple exercise like tapping your finger on the table is causing your brain to re-wire itself. Now, imagine what happens when you start messing with memory. Every component, the nerve cells, the synapses, the dendrites, are all dependent upon the other. And our brain forms memories in such a way that it is all inter-connected. So if you mess with one memory…"

"You mess up all of them." Marty finished, starting to grasp what Ben was saying.

"This is what is happening to you now. What should be routine and subconscious isn't anymore. It is very much like your brain reaching into a drawer for something it expects to be there, only to find the drawer empty."

"Or looking for where a drawer used to be, but it's been relocated or eliminated altogether." Marty added.

"Right. Memory is an interconnected process. You cannot mess with one memory, without eventually messing with them all. What you have done is tip the first domino. It's only a matter of time before the rest of them fall. Unless you're able to remember what you erased."

Marty stared off into the distance, unable to fully process what was happening to him. How could all of the memories he had built up over the years go away?

"But what about the hours I'm missing leading up to the procedure? How did he erase those?"

"Yes, that part is a bit more difficult to understand. My only guess is he also figured out a way to target and eliminate the most recent connections that had been formed. It seems crazy to think about, but so does all of this. If he had the knowledge to locate and eliminate the unique connections tying you to your most painful memory, then it's not a stretch to think he could find the most recent connections and eliminate them as well. Even if you concede that point, it's hard to comprehend why he chose four hours and how he was able to keep it to such a specific period of time."

"It's hard to comprehend any of it. Even understanding a little of the science behind what's happening, it's still a mystery. All of it."

"Absolutely. Even in all of my reading, everything I've learned, everything I've lost, I still have so many questions. Still so much that eludes me. It took way too long to figure out what was happening to me. By the time I realized it and started journaling, it unraveled so quickly, before I even got the chance to do anything about it. One morning I sat on the patio of a home I had no recollection of building, sipping black coffee and wondering what in the hell happened to my life."

Ben sat there, momentarily lost in thought.

"It was then I knew, I had to find the Professor," he finally said.

"To confront him, to get your memory back?"

"Initially, yes. I did everything I could to talk to him. I banged on his door. Never an answer. I watched the home where he lived. He never seemed to come and go. There were times I knew he was there, the lights in the house were on, there was a silhouette or silhouettes in the window. Then the house would grow dark for hours, sometimes days at a time. I guess he would leave and come back while I was napping, but how did that happen every single time? It's like he knew I was watching him. I don't know how, and maybe I'm wrong, but he had to have known."

"So what did you do?"

"I finally realized I was never going to get to him. I knew what he had done, what I had chosen, was permanent. If I couldn't confront him, if I couldn't help myself recover, I decided the next best thing was to keep tabs on him so I could help the next person whom he encountered. Try to convince them to change their mind. To warn them about the dangers of going through with it. I watched the house for weeks, waiting for someone to walk up the driveway to his doorstep with a box in hand.

There was only one afternoon I was gone for an extended period from the house. I went to the grocery pick up some food, some batteries, and beer. It was raining lightly, and I had forgotten my umbrella in the car. When I got back to my VW bug, I realized I had locked my keys in the car. So there I was, in the mist, locked out of my own vehicle. Some detective I turned out to be. I had to wait for a tow truck to come let me in my car. By the time I got back to my stakeout spot, I arrived just in time to see someone walking into the house. Turned out to be you. It was too late to intervene before the procedure. My only option was to wait and find you afterward. I'm here to help you. I want you to have a different outcome than I did. I want to help you save and restore your memory."

"How long do I have?" Marty asked, afraid of the answer.

Ben responded, matter-of-factly. "Ten days. Two weeks at most. Maybe a day more, maybe a day or two less. For me, it was about day twelve when I knew my memory was gone. From that day forward, I only retained new memories.

"Oh my God. There's got to be a way to stop this. What do I do?" Marty said, panic in his voice.

"Write down a list of significant moments in your life, as far back as you can think. Your first recollection as a child, a significant moment from elementary school, a scene from your favorite family vacation, a fight you got into in middle school, your first kiss, your first day of high school, the day you got your first car, your high school graduation, your college roommates, etc. As much as you can remember now. List them in chronological order with the most recent at the top and number them all the way down until you get to the oldest memory, whatever it is."

"Why?"

"This is going to act as a clock of sorts. The erasure of your memory is working from your oldest memories all the way up to the most recent, until eventually it is wiped clean, like taking a magnet to a credit card. In this case, the magnet is starting with your oldest memories and working it's way forward."

"I don't quite understand what you mean."

"Basically, this is the time we have to find the Professor and figure out what memory he erased. If we can somehow get him to restore the memory he erased, my theory is all of the other connections will be restored as well. And hopefully you'll recover your full memory."

"And if we don't? If we can't find the Professor, or if he can't help us?"

"If we get to the point where you can't remember the last thing on the list, your most recent memory before the procedure, it will be too late. Your long-term memory will be lost. Forever."

"I can't believe this."

"I know. If I hadn't experienced it myself, I wouldn't have believed it, either. But I'm telling you, this is going to happen if you don't do something about it. And we need this list to give us an idea how exactly how much time we have to figure it out."

Memory is everything, Marty remembered the Professor telling him. "So much of who I am, the richness of human experience and existence, is tied to the things I remember. My family, my friends, the experiences making me the person I am today. It's all tied up in my memory. If I lose it, I lose my relationships, my education, my faith. If I lose it all, I lose me. I can't believe I ever agreed to letting that Mad Scientist mess with my head. He deceived me!"

"No, he didn't deceive you."

Marty shot an apoplectic look at Ben. "Yes. He did. He never said any of this was going to happen. He never mentioned side effects."

"Did you ask?"

Marty fell silent. No, he hadn't asked. How could he not have asked?

"If you were like me, you were so desperate to get rid of one memory it clouded your thinking. Nothing else mattered but finding relief, finding peace. We race past a lot of important questions when we're desperate."

"What kind of questions?"

"Questions like 'What is the purpose of this memory and this pain?' 'What can I learn from it?' 'What past experiences have I had that could give me perspective?' 'Would I really go back and undo this if I could? 'What would it lead to if I did?' We bury these thoughts when all we can think about is the pain, the loss, the regret. Regret is the most helpless feeling of all. Nothing in the world can alleviate the sting of wishing we could go back and do it differently, and knowing we just can't."

It was true what Ben was saying. Marty knew it. He didn't like it, but he knew it. Maybe he could trust Ben.

Trust was a rare commodity in his life right now. He didn't know why he felt he might be able to trust him, perhaps it was the bond they shared having both made the same mistake. Whatever it was, he was grateful it seemed he was no longer alone in this mess. And, man, was it ever a mess. How were they going to find the Professor? And if they couldn't, were there other ways to trigger his memory? What was it that was so awful he was willing to ignore all of the warnings in his soul and subject himself to such a risky procedure? He was going to find out. And Ben was going to help him. He had to believe that.

If he didn't believe it, he would have no reason to go on.

~~~ ~~~ ~~~ ~~~ ~~~ ~~~ ~~~

From Marty's List of Memories

First day in my new apartment. I cooked steaks on the grill for my sister, her husband, and me. We drank red wine and she told me about her first experience moving out. I slept on the sofa because my new bed hadn't been delivered yet. Woke up with a slight hangover and missed my early class.

The day I wrecked my Jeep. Totaled it before I had even made three payments on it. Took it too fast around a curve one spring night and clipped a tree. I suffered a lot of cuts and bruises and broke my wrist. But I was much more upset about losing the Jeep. Without any backup plan or savings, I was back to a bike.

The day I bought my Jeep. It was a Saturday morning. My brother-in-law, who sells cars for a living, drove it to my apartment. I paid him cash and signed all of the appropriate paperwork. I dropped him off at his office and took the jeep outside the city. Up a stretch of road that winds alongside a river. I was gone all day. Weather was perfect. Top down, music up. Bliss.

Sister's college graduation. She made it. I was so proud of her, but man it was hot in that auditorium.

First day of college. Didn't get the class I wanted, so I waited outside the drop/add office for a few hours until someone dropped, opening up a spot for me. I had dinner with some people from my Biology class at a pizza place downtown. The server was cute, and aggressive. She hit on me, which I loved. I asked for her number, but I never called.

Summer after senior year. Worked in a warehouse for a shipping company. Went to the beach with some friends from school, kissed a girl I'd had a crush on for over a year, but nothing developed because she went overseas. I went to Panama with a non-profit group and distributed food, clothing, and medical supplies to families living in such poverty it made me sick to my stomach. I left there saying I would come back every summer. Still haven't gone back.

Graduation day. Practice in the morning. Breakfast buffet. Navy blue cap and gown. We each gave the principal a paper clip as he shook our hand. We threw our hats in the air. I felt happy and sad, but free. Oh how I wished my grandfather had lived long enough to see it. I went out with some friends for a while, but had to be home at a decent hour. I had gotten the flu the day I was to take the SAT and so I had to make it up the morning after graduation. Miserable.

My grandfather's death. 3 weeks before my high school graduation.

Senior Prom. Couldn't afford a limo. The only car available was my parents' older model sedan. It was a 5-speed. My father had tried to teach me several times, but finally lost his patience. I don't blame him. I was stubborn and hard to teach sometimes. Under pressure, with no choice, I took the car out in the cul-de-sac in front of my parents' house and in 3 hours taught myself to drive it. That evening, with my best friend and his date in the back seat, I drove the four of us downtown to a restaurant and then to the dance at a hotel. I only stalled out twice.

Junior Prom. Flunked my driver's license test (trend) on the morning of Prom. Had to take my date in a cab to Prom. Afterward, I tried for several minutes, unsuccessfully, to obtain a ride home for my date and me until a friend who lived down the street took pity on me and drove us home. Never had another date with her again and some of my football teammates called me "taxi boy" for a while.

Eagle Scout ceremony. My father was so proud. I was just glad to get it over with. Wish I had appreciated it more at the time.

Dad's heart attack. He was young. Only 39. Most people don't survive. He did. He changed that day. Not just in what he ate and how often he exercised, but how he treated my sister and me. He was much more loving and open and expressive from then on.

15 years old. Flunked my driving permit test. Humiliating. "Did you even read the book?" The police officer at the DMV has asked me condescendingly, as if I were wasting his and everyone else's time. I

hadn't even looked at the book. My Dad took me back a week later, after I had studied like crazy, and I got every question right.

First kiss. Annie Walker. At almost 16 years old, I was the last of my friend group to have a first kiss. I was a late bloomer. Always a late bloomer.

First varsity football start. Sophomore year. I played tight end. The exhilaration as I took the field. The pride I felt. I got whipped pretty good a few times by a senior defensive end. But I caught two passes and we won the game when the other team missed a last second field goal.

First day of high school. It was so big. Overwhelming. Got lost twice. Forgot my locker combination. Survived, if just barely.

Fight at the bus stop. Bully was picking on a weaker kid because he played the flute in the band. I stood in between the bully and the flute player and took home a fat lip for my trouble.

13 years old. Sailing on the lake with my grandfather. He taught me how to sail.

My beloved dog, Charlie the Cocker Spaniel, died. I was 12. We buried him in the back yard.

Brought a lunch box to school on the first day of 6th grade. Nobody told me it wasn't socially acceptable in middle school. Got made fun of. Came home, threw the lunch box away, went to my room and cried.

Got a brand new bike for Christmas 4th grade year. Rode it the entire day.

Trip to Disney World in 2nd grade. I was in love with Snow White. As her float passed by in the parade I just stared at her, mesmerized. One day I will marry Snow White, I thought.

First night spending the night away from home. At my grandparents' house. I was terrified and homesick. They had a multi-colored light that spun and projected the sparkling images on the wall. It distracted me enough to where I could fall asleep.

Got separated from my parents in a department store. I looked up and suddenly they were gone. I was all alone. Not really, though. There were many people around, just nobody that mattered to me. I had never known what it felt like to be lonely until that moment. Terrified, I found a person with a name tag and they called my parents over the store intercom.

Theme song from the show I watched every morning as a kid would pop into my head at various and random times. I still remembered every word. How could I still remember every word?

Chapter Eight

"The best way to find out if you can trust somebody is to trust them." - Ernest Hemingway

Marty and Ben slowly walked back to where they started. It was only then Marty realized he never let Joe know he wasn't going to be at work. He pulled his cell phone out of his pocket and there were four missed calls from the coffee shop. The last one was from about an hour before. Joe had finally given up. *Great. There goes my job. Oh well. More time to get all of this figured out, I suppose.*

"Earlier you said you had been watching the Professor's house, right?" Marty said, something dawning on him for the first time.

"Yep. I was there twenty-four seven until you left. Haven't been back since I started tracking you down."

"So you can take me there? You can lead me back to his house. I can talk to him, get him to undo this."

"Possibly."

"What do you mean, 'possibly'?"

"I don't know if he will see you. Don't know if he will want to help. Don't know if it's even a reversible procedure. There are a lot of unknowns. But I'll take you there. It's as good a place to start as any."

"Great. Can we go right now?

96

"Sure can. Hop in and we'll roll."

"Okay, let me make a quick phone call."

Ben made his way around to the driver's seat of the orange VW, unlocked the door, and climbed inside while Marty took a moment to try and reach Joe at work. There was no answer, so he just left a voicemail saying some unforeseen circumstances had come up (true) and that his phone had died (lie) and he was so sorry and he hoped Joe would understand. As he hung up, he thought, *no way he's gonna understand.* He placed the phone in his pocket and jumped in the passenger seat next to Ben. He buckled his seat belt as Ben put the car in gear and cranked the engine. It slowly came to life and they headed off in the direction of the Professor's house.

"Are we just going to pull up in the driveway?" Marty asked.

"What do you mean?"

"I mean, do you think it is best if we sneak up to the door instead, you know, in case the Professor is in the middle of a procedure, or he doesn't want to see us?"

"Oh, no, we most definitely won't be pulling up in the driveway. If he's even there, the only way we have any chance of catching him in person is to sneak up to the house…and force our way in."

"Like criminals? Man. I have no idea how to break and enter. You?"

"Why do you think I never did it? I've never broken a law in my life. Plus, it was always just me, ya know? Two might not be a lot, but it's double what I was without you. 'Strength in numbers,' they say."

"So you've had a lot of time to think this through, though. You obviously had to have come up with some ideas about what you would do if you ever found me, or whoever the Professor's next patient was going to be."

"Well, yeah, I thought about it."

"And?"

"And, I have a crowbar under the hood up there. I was thinking we sneak up to the back door and try to pry it open."

"That's it?"

"Listen, I'm not a professional thief. I'm sure I had some street knowledge at some point before I started losing my memory. But I'm not operating with a full deck, here, remember. You have to cut me some slack. Do you have a better idea?"

"No. Not really. But what if he's armed? What if there's an alarm or a guard dog? We have no protection for ourselves."

"I don't know. We'll have to figure all of this out on the fly. Let's just hope none of those things are true. I mean, we have to catch a break at some point or another, don't we?"

"Maybe."

"Maybe is good enough for me. So here's what we'll do." Ben started, as he made his way down the poplar-lined streets leading away from downtown. "I'll park the car where I normally would and we will go through the woods to the place I've been observing from this whole time. From there, we can get a feel for how and when to proceed. If it looks like nobody is home, we will wait, all night if we have to. Then we'll slowly make our way from opposite sides of the yard and meet up at the back door. I'll do the honors with the crowbar. I've got a flashlight in here somewhere, probably on the floorboard back there."

Marty turned around and felt around until he located it under Ben's seat. "Got it."

"Good. I'll be on crowbar, you'll be on flashlight. With those two weapons, we can't lose, right?" Marty forced a chuckle at Ben's attempt at lightening the mood. "Anyway, if all of this works like we want it to, once we're inside the house, we go from room to room until we find a real person, hopefully the Professor. He tells you how to get your original memory back, I punch him in the gut, and we walk out of there both getting what we want."

"That's all you want is to inflict a little physical pain on him? You're a better man than me."

"Nah. I actually wouldn't even do that. I'm a lover, not a fighter. I'm not really a lover, either. It's complicated."

Marty was still trying to get used to Ben's sense of humor, if that's what it was. Maybe he was just quirky. Or maybe Marty just wasn't in the mood to joke right now. He did appreciate the effort though, and one day might come to appreciate this quality. One day. But it was only earlier today he even realized Ben was trying to help him. And he still couldn't be completely sure. What if he was leading him into a trap? What if all of this was some elaborate scheme put in motion by the Professor himself, to ensure Marty didn't talk about what happened to him? That didn't make sense on any level. Maybe Ben was just crazy. Maybe he has lured strangers into the woods before. The thought made gave Marty chills. No, he knew too much, was too connected to the situation, the things he said too accurate for that to be the case.

Right?

The car suddenly veered off the main road onto a gravel path. After a few hundred yards, Ben slowed to a stop in an open field that abutted some woods on the north and east sides of the field. It was dusk. The sun had already dipped below the horizon to the west. Marty rolled his window down and heard the symphony of crickets, and frogs, and millions of other bugs and creatures. "The Professor's house is on the other side of those woods," Ben said and pointed past Marty to the dense area of trees to his right.

"How far?"

"No more than a half mile."

Marty noticed he was wearing the shoes he normally wore to work. Brown Sperry's. *Great. Perfect hiking shoes to go with the golf shirt and khakis I'm sporting.*

"You've got the flashlight, right?"

Marty lifted it from the space between his legs with a look communicating "check!"

"Alright, I'll grab the crowbar and then we are all set. I've got some snacks and beverages and other supplies stashed at the stakeout location."

Emerging from the car, Ben popped the hood of the car while Marty waited with the flashlight. It was weird seeing no engine under the hood of the older-model vehicle. Marty remembered his grandfather explaining to him how a VW Bug's engine was in the back of the car, making the front the storage area, but he had never looked under the hood of one before. *At least I remember the conversation,* Marty thought. Ben came to his side and said, "Alright, we're ready to go." Marty looked up at the sky. It was gray, with pillowed clouds layered on top of one another as far as the eye could see. The sun was below the horizon. Daylight was lingering now, holding on for dear life. It wouldn't be long before darkness took over.

~~~ ~~~ ~~~ ~~~ ~~~ ~~~ ~~~

Darkness had taken over the city. Marty and Jane were eating dinner together at a cafe owned by a long-time friend of Jane's family. Her sister Joy, just 16

months younger, was working as a hostess. She greeted them and showed them to a table. Marty had only met her once before. She was very similar physically to Jane, similar height, same eyes and smile. Where Jane was introverted, Joy was the life of the party. Working as a hostess was an ideal fit for her personality.

It was unusually warm for a late February evening and Joy, at their request, sat them outside at a metal table with an umbrella in the center. She said, "please enjoy your meal" as if she didn't know them personally, and excused herself. A server quickly came by and set two glasses of water on the table. And it wasn't long before the condensation from the cups began intermittently dripping through the holes in the table. Just a few feet away, a man, late-twenties, in a cabbie hat, tight-fitting print tee shirt, and gray skinny jeans played *Let It Be* on his guitar.

Marty paid no attention to neither the song nor the moisture from the water glass accumulating in the same spot on one leg of his jeans. He was in another world. A world where the only things in existence were the brightness of Jane's eyes and the timbre of her voice. He was mesmerized, and he was at a point of confidence in the relationship where he didn't even try to hide it anymore. He was falling fast, the beat of his heart syncing with the rhythm of her breathing.

As he sat there listening to her talk about art and faith and the meaning of life, he realized he had never met anyone who was as grounded and self-aware as she was. People figure out who they are at all different ages, some are very young, some are in life's twilight, and some never figure it out at all. Jane knew exactly who she was at age twenty-one. He envied her, and he longed to know her even better than she knew herself. Somewhere on a subconscious level, cords of emotion, attraction, and affinity were winding together, growing ever stronger by the minute.

When the man playing guitar broke into *Hey Jude*, Jane said "You know my little brother's name is Judah, and my father used to sing him this song when we were little, making a big deal about the extra syllable at the end of his name. My siblings and I would just crack up every time…" And her words trailed off as her eyes wandered off into some distant, sad, unexplored place. He wanted to probe, to go into that place with her and make it okay, but instead he went with changing the subject.

"Your siblings all have the same first initials?"

"Yes. We're all J's. I didn't really see the purpose of it when I was younger, but now I think it's kind of cool. You and your sister have the same first initial, too!"

"Yep, and we have identical middle initials as well. I'm Martin Donald and she is Melody Danielle."

"That's so cool. I *love* it," Jane said, as she zoned out again momentarily, her thoughts drifting away with the music.

Just as he was about to say something, she came back from her momentary trance, took a sip of her water, and said, "I wonder if it's even possible, to 'take a sad song and make it better.' You know, like they sing in *Hey Jude*."

I will spend the rest of my days taking all of your sad songs and making them better, Marty thought. What he said out loud was, "Of course it is. But you can't do it alone." She smiled a genuine smile and grabbed his hand. "Maybe someday I'll find someone to collaborate with," she responded, still smiling. Marty felt the message in her smile as it ran white hot through his bloodstream and straight to his heart.

~~~ ~~~ ~~~ ~~~ ~~~ ~~~ ~~~

Marty couldn't help but feel unsettled as he thought about being in unfamiliar woods with someone he barely knew. And that was the easier part. Was he really about to invade a person's home? It's remarkable how one decision can send a life spiraling out of control. If he could have seen it play out before he made his choice, surely he would have backed out. Whatever he wanted to forget, it couldn't be worth what it had already cost. Not to mention the toll it may still inflict.

"This way," was all Ben said to get them started. Marty followed behind as they entered the wooded area through an opening about eighty yards from where they parked the car. The light was immediately vanished under the canopy of trees. It was a bit startling how quickly it happened. The lack of light made Marty's abdominal muscles tighten even more and the juices in his stomach were beginning to roil. About one hundred feet in, Ben broke the silence. In a whisper, he said, "I guess it doesn't make sense for you to carry the flashlight now since I'm the one who knows where I'm going. Give me the flashlight now and you hold the crowbar. We can switch back when we get to the stakeout spot." *Why are you whispering? We've got to be the only ones out here.* He hesitated giving up control of the flashlight until it dawned on him the crowbar provided more protection.

With the flashlight in hand, Ben picked up the pace. Marty, unfamiliar with the terrain and not being able to see very well in front of him, was doing his best to keep up. *What's your hurry?! Slow down!* Marty thought, but he remained silent and tried to stay in Ben's footsteps. It was obvious he had spent some time in these woods. *Who spends time in woods? Crazy people, that's who.* Marty started adding things up in his head. *Guy stalks you. Guy stalks you until you relent and talk to him. Guy who stalked you talks you into getting into his car. Guy who stalked you convinces you to ride with him to a remote area. Guy who stalks you then leads you into dense woods at night. I've got to be the dumbest guy alive.*

At least I have the crowbar.

In the midst of this last thought, Marty felt his right foot fall on a large root sticking out of the ground, unseen. His ankle rolled, and, because of the brisk pace, he pitched forward, arms flailing out in front of him to brace for impact. The crowbar came flying out of his hands as he landed hard on the floor of the woods, striking his elbow on a rock on the way down. His face hit after his hands and a combination of dirt and leaves and probably bugs entered into his open mouth as he was shouting for Ben to stop.

Marty rolled over onto his back. His ankle was throbbing. He instinctively reached to check his left elbow and he could feel the blood and open wound. He couldn't see anything. "Ben!" He called again. "Ben, I need help!"

Where is he? He has to know I'm not behind him. What the hell is taking so long?

Marty waited there, in the darkness, which felt like it was moving down upon him, pressing him down into the dirt of the woods.

Suddenly a light clicked on behind him. Marty twisted his torso around and looked up into the bright light. He saw the familiar flannel shirt and the beard.

It was Ben.

In one hand was the flashlight.

In his other hand he clutched the crowbar.

Chapter Nine

"There are things known and things unknown and in between are the doors." - Jim Morrison

Marty just sat there, unsure what was going to happen next. He half-expected Ben to bring the crowbar down onto his head. He could bury him right here. Nice and tidy. Probably has a shovel under the hood of that VW Bug, too. *Not your brightest move, Marty. Not by a long-shot. You idiot.*

The light from the flashlight flickered and went out. Marty could hear Ben smacking it. "Damn thing," he said. "Batteries must be going dead. Always check the batteries, Ben. You idiot." *Wait, that's my line,* thought Marty. Suddenly, the flashlight clicked back on and Ben bent down beside Marty. "What happened? I was moving along and all of a sudden you weren't there. I heard you yell, but I was already a good ways in front of you. Then this thing decided to go out," he said, waving the flashlight.

"Man, you really jacked yourself up, huh?"

"Yeah, I guess I did. Somewhere in the dark over there is a root that's a real nasty S.O.B. It jumped right up and tripped me out of nowhere. Rolled my ankle pretty good. Then a rock was kind enough to appear and open up a wound on my left elbow to balance things out."

"Let me have a look at you."

Ben turned the light down on to Marty's ankle and studied it for a moment. At some point in his life, he may have known something about what to do when a person sprains their ankle. If he did, it was knowledge lost in the thick haze that had slowly and methodically wiped out most of his memory. It made him feel helpless, and it stirred anger inside him. Anger he felt many times every day. Each time he experienced something he couldn't remember. Sure, he had made a nice little speech to Marty about how it wasn't the Professor's fault, that it was their choice to do this. That they brought it upon themselves. But he didn't really believe it. At least not completely. And he knew Marty didn't really, either. The Professor had knowledge that he, they, didn't have. He should have been more forthcoming about the unintended consequences. He shouldn't be messing with people's memories, with their brains, with their lives. He shouldn't be allowed…

"Well, what's the diagnosis, nurse? Is it swollen? You're blocking my view."

Marty's question brought Ben back from his thoughts. "Yeah, it looks a little tender, but nothing too serious. Let me wrap it up somehow and then we'll get you on your feet and see if you can put any pressure on it. We've got to try to get you out of here. This isn't the place you want to hang around for a long time."

"No kidding. But what are you going to wrap it with?"

Ben stood up and removed his long sleeve shirt. With the sharp end of the crowbar, he attempted to tear it.

"Whoa, wait a minute," Marty objected. "Don't ruin your shirt!"

"This old thing? I've got twenty more exactly like it in my closet."

Marty couldn't see Ben's face really well at the moment, but he was sure he had a playful smile on his face. He could sense it. After working with it for a few moments, Marty heard a tearing sound and Ben's voice saying "finally" under his breath. When he had torn one of the sleeves completely off, he bent down again and handed Marty the crowbar. "Hold this. You can clamp your teeth down on it if this becomes really painful." Marty grabbed the crowbar and set it down under his right hand while Ben lifted his leg and began to wrap it with the fabric from his shirt. The procedure was painful, but not terribly so. Marty winced every now and then, but he was careful not to jerk his foot or to make a show of his pain. He didn't want Ben to feel bad.

~~~ ~~~ ~~~ ~~~ ~~~ ~~~ ~~~

Jane winced as Marty applied the ice pack to her swollen left ankle. "It's so cold," she said. "I know, Baby. I'm really sorry." Marty reassured her. He took off the white t-shirt he was wearing and used it to keep the ankle stable and the ice in place. He was shirtless now, sweat dripping down his chest, the waist of his boxers peeking out over the top of his khaki shorts as he knelt beside her. This outing had not gone at all like he hoped it would.

They were only about a mile into a 3-mile hike when Marty asked Jane if she was getting tired, perhaps she needed a piggy-back ride? "I don't need a ride, but maybe *you* do." she said.

"You couldn't carry me 2 feet without collapsing."

"Oh yeah? Try me. I'll carry you all through these woods and back."

Marty tried to laugh it off and continue, but she stopped. When he looked back Jane had this look on her face as if to say "I'm not going any further until I prove this to you."

He shook his head and reluctantly marched back to where she was and got behind her.

"This is not going to work," he said as he attempted to hop onto her back. Although he was lithe and she was athletic, his 6' 3" frame was a bit much for her 5'6". The first couple of times she failed to grab a hold of his legs and he just flopped back down. On the third attempt, she caught his legs behind the knees and he raised up to position himself better.

"You ready back there?"

"Ready. I guess."

And off they went.

Turned out Marty was wrong. They had made it several hundred feet before Jane's foot found a discreet rock causing her to roll over her ankle, pitching them both forward in a heap. Marty instinctively braced himself on his forearms so the full force of his weight wouldn't land on Jane and rolled off to the side.

When he turned over to look at her, she was laughing.

"Oh, man, I really screwed that up." It wasn't a laugh of joy, but an awkward laugh, a laugh to hide the embarrassment.

"Are you okay?" Marty asked, too concerned to share in the laugh.

"My ego is wounded, and my ankle hurts like crazy. Other than that I'm perfectly fine." Jane joked in spite of the pain.

Marty quickly took his backpack off and retrieved the first aid kit. He pulled out the ice pack and cracked it to release the chemicals. It turned cold instantly in his hands. After he finished wrapping it, he helped her stand up and put the backpack on her shoulders. Leaning down in front of her, he helped her hop on his back and began to carry her the mile or so back to the place they parked.

Despite the difficulty of the hike carrying extra weight, Marty didn't mind. He hated Jane was hurting, but he loved the fact that he was rescuing her. Pulling her out of the woods, doing for her what she couldn't do for herself. He loved holding on to her thighs, which were silky soft with the tone of a swimmer. He could feel her breasts beneath the tank top she was wearing as she pressed up against his bare back, her arms flung around his neck, connected at the wrists. She smelled so good, even though she had been sweating. Her breath on his neck warm and sweet. He felt like he could carry her around the world and back.

I may be saving you physically, but you're saving me in every other way. You've pulled my heart out of the dark woods, you're carrying it home.

~~~ ~~~ ~~~ ~~~ ~~~ ~~~ ~~~

As Ben was finishing up the wrap job, Marty noticed the t-shirt he had been wearing under the long-sleeve flannel. It was a dark shirt, probably black, with bright orange lettering on the back reading *Pierce Construction.*

"Alright, maybe that will keep the swelling at bay until we can get to some ice. Let's try to get you up and see if you can make it out of here without making it worse."

Ben reached down and offered Marty his hand. Marty reached up with his right hand and grabbed ahold of it. With surprising strength, Ben did most of the work swiftly pulling Marty up off of the ground. Marty was upright now. He gingerly placed his right foot on the ground next to his left and slowly tried to put his weight on it. He was relieved to find he was able to walk with a limp. It was a significant limp, but at least it wasn't the worst case scenario.

"How is it?" Ben asked.

"It's okay. Definitely hurting, but I think I can make a go of it." Marty said.

"Okay, good. Just to be safe, I'll walk right beside you. If you need to rest or lean against me at any time, just let me know. We'll go slow from here on out," Ben said as they began to walk.

Marty remembered he had left the crowbar on the ground.

"Wait a second. I forgot the crowbar."

"Oh. Yeah. I'll get it." Ben said, using the flashlight to locate it. He rejoined Marty, handing him the tool. Marty grabbed it with his right hand and they began to move toward their destination again. As they walked, well, as Ben walked and Marty shuffled, Marty asked him about the shirt he was wearing.

"I noticed your shirt says Pierce Construction on the back. That your company?"

"Yep. Well, *was* my company. I lost it. Hard to maintain a business when all of your knowledge about the business disappears."

"I'm sorry. That must have been really difficult."

"It was. I remember each of those moments when something I was supposed to know had vanished from my mind. Getting a question from a worker, talking with a client on a job site, negotiating a price with a sub-contractor. It was frustrating, embarrassing, terrifying all at the same time. Over the course of days and weeks and months, my employees lost faith in me, and my credibility with clients and sub-contractors had whittled away to almost nothing. Ultimately, I decided selling the business was not only in my best interest, but in the best interest of everyone involved."

"I can't imagine how hard that must have been. I'm sorry."

"Yeah. Me, too. Sold it to my right-hand man. So at least I knew it was in good hands. And I got a little money out of the deal so I didn't have to worry about where the paycheck would come from for a while. So it's not a total disaster, anyway. But it sure feels like it sometimes. Feelings and reality are often at odds with one another."

I hope that's true, because you're giving my emotions a serious batch of mixed signals, thought Marty. He hobbled alongside Ben for what seemed like another hour or so, the woods becoming darker by the minute. Animal noises peppered the area. Some were bugs and birds, but some sounded much more menacing. Marty tried not to focus on those. No way he could outrun a dangerous animal in his condition. Snakes were another matter. He could step on one at any time. He pushed those thoughts out of his mind and concentrated on the task at hand. His ankle was throbbing now. He needed ice and ibuprofen. Probably wasn't going to get it anytime soon. Not a pleasant realization. It got even more unpleasant as his face met with a rather large spider web Ben had somehow managed to miss. Marty spit and began furiously wiping his face and hair with his free hand. *Probably have a huge, poisonous spider crawling down my shirt now.*

"You ok?" Ben asked, stopping and pointing the flashlight in Marty's direction.

"Yeah, just took out an enormous spider web with my face, but I'm fine."

"Oh, I meant your ankle."

"Right. Well, it hurts pretty good, but I'm ok. Hey, shine that light on my shoulders and back and make sure I don't have a spider on me."

"Ok." Ben said, chuckling. "I think you're good. Won't be much longer now. We should see the house through the trees pretty soon if there is any light on."

They walked another few hundred feet and a light appeared up ahead, just as Ben had said.

"There it is," Ben said. "Just inside the edge of the woods, I've got a camping chair you can sit in while we wait and re-group."

Marty got an uneasy feeling in his stomach as the trees thinned out and the silhouette of the house became clearer against the night sky. *So this was the place where I made the worst decision of my life.* Marty was back at the place he blew it. It was a surreal experience, a mix of equal parts anxiety and clarity. He wondered why he didn't see clearer before. Anger and shame came knocking at the door of Marty's heart. But he chose not to answer. The pain in his ankle combined with his determination to make things right overshadowed his negative impulses for the moment. He was ready to confront this guy, bad wheel and all.

They made their way over to the stakeout spot and Marty maneuvered himself around to the front of the chair and plopped down. Ben fetched a cooler from behind a tree. "I've got apples, beer and water in here, but the beer is lukewarm, at best."

"Water sounds amazing, thanks."

Ben grabbed a water for Marty and a beer for himself. Sensing that Marty was giving him a strange look, he put the flashlight up to his face and gave an "oh well" expression combined with a shrug and popped open the can. He took a big swig and then positioned the cooler at Marty's feet and helped him to prop his leg up on it.

"Thanks, I appreciate it," Marty said, opening his bottle of water and taking a long pull on it. Water never tasted so good.

Ben crouched down beside the chair and cut the flashlight off. Marty could hear him chug the rest of the can of beer and toss it down on the ground beside him. "House is quieter than usual. Not many lights on and I can't see any shadows on the other side of the windows." Ben was talking like a man with experience. *How many nights had he sat here in this camping chair by himself, just waiting to get another glimpse of the Professor? If he never had any luck, what difference was another person going to make? Especially one whose movement was now significantly limited.*

"He's either not at home or asleep. Too early for him to be asleep. He's probably out looking for his next patient. Another desperate life ready to sell its soul for a little peace."

Marty noticed a change in tone when Ben would talk about the Professor. It was subtle, but it was there. At first, he seemed neutral, almost even defending the man. The more comfortable he became with Marty, the more his tone and statements developed a bit of an edge. It made Marty wonder for the first time, just who was helping whom.

"We'll wait about another thirty minutes. Give you a chance to rest your leg and to see if there's any movement in the house. It's almost 9. At 9:30, we'll make a break for the back door, assuming you're okay to move."

"Aye aye, cap'n."

The thirty minutes seemed to take forever. They sat there in silence, both of them transfixed on the house. Ben polishing off another three cans of warm beer, disappearing a couple of times to relieve himself in the woods, while Marty sat there and tried to visualize what was about to happen. Was he really about to break into someone's house? *What if this isn't even the Professor's house? What if this is Ben's ex-wife's house or a former business partner who owes him money?* What they were about to do was illegal, and that was bad enough. He didn't want to add abetting a relative stranger's bad motives on top of it. He reminded himself how crazy it was the amount of trust he was putting in a man he knew so little about.

Then he remembered the Memory List. He could feel the journal wedged in between the waist of this shorts and the skin of his back. He reached behind him and pulled it out, opening it to the list he had written on the first page only hours before. Holding the flashlight between his shoulder blade and chin, his eyes went down the list all the way to the earliest memory and his heart sank when he tried to recall what he had written on the page. It was gone. There in his mind just a little while ago, and now vanished as if someone had erased it with a pencil. It was happening. Already. Discouraged, he put the journal back where he got it from and reminded himself this was the reason he was here right now. He had to put a stop to this, and soon.

"It's 9:30. Nothing has changed as far as I can see. You ready to do this?"

"Ready or not, here we are. Let's move."

Ben popped up from beside the chair and offered Marty his hand. Marty grabbed it, putting weight on his good foot first. Then he slowly brought a little bit of his weight on his right foot, anticipating the worst. He was relieved when he could place enough of his body weight on it to limp on his own. It still hurt pretty badly, but he was young and he always had a high tolerance for pain. Ben handed him the flashlight and Marty shined it on the ground, locating the crow bar. Ben picked it up and they both took a deep breath at the same time.

This was happening.

Marty guessed there were about one hundred yards of open space they would have to cover before they reached the back of the house. *Stealth for the length of an entire football field with a sprained ankle? Sure. Why not.*

Ben looked at Marty. "You need me to support any of your weight?"

"Let's see if I can get there on my own. It won't be quick, but I think I can do it.'

"Alright, sir. Your call."

Without any further words, Ben set out across the field of knee-high grass sitting between the woods and the official edge of the property line, where the grass would be cut and they would be more exposed if anyone was watching. *If anyone was watching.* The thought sent a chill up Marty's spine and goosebumps broke out on his skin as he limped along, bending as low as possible in the mixture of tall grass and weeds. He was just praying he didn't step on anything else. Each stride was careful, deliberate, but focused and determined. He felt he might be just a few hundred feet away from some answers to this dilemma and that thought, combined with the fear of being caught, sent much-needed adrenaline coursing through his veins.

When they reached the yard, Ben stopped and squatted down at the edge of the property line. Marty limped up in a few seconds and did his best to squat down next to him. Although it wasn't much of a squat. He just lowered his upper frame and placed his hands on his knees. From this closer vantage point, they watched the house for a few more moments - just to be sure. When it was clear there was no movement coming from in or around the house, they crossed over into the yard and crept the last fifteen yards or so up to the back door.

There was a small concrete square, a patio of sorts, just outside the back door. Ben sat down on one side of the door, while Marty took his place at the other. They were both breathing heavy, big beads of sweat forming on their foreheads and then running down their cheeks. Turns out criminal activity was stressful business.

As they sat there, regrouping and attempting to summon whatever courage each of them had remaining in the tank, the stillness of the evening gave way to a faint sound coming from inside the house. They both heard it at the same time and looked at each other with curious faces. It could be the sound of the TV, which was unnerving. Sure, a lot of people leave the television on for various reasons when they leave the house, because they forget or because they want some noise in the house in case intruders get any ideas. Suddenly that logic made perfect sense. It was certainly giving Marty and Ben pause.

They looked at each other again. It was too late to turn back now. They had come too far. Marty nodded at Ben and Ben nodded back. He moved over closer to Marty and positioned himself in front of the door near the handle while Marty shined the flashlight. Ben slid the long end of the crowbar as far into the opening between the door and the doorjamb as he could. Satisfied that it was wedged in enough not to move, he went to reposition himself to get the most leverage when the crowbar came loose from the door. Ben realized it and reached out to try and stop it. Marty saw it falling, but just a little too late. By the time his brain recognized what was happening and instructed him to react, his arms didn't have time to get in position. He lunged forward to no avail, and felt Ben falling over on top of him attempting to do the same. The crowbar fell to the concrete with a series of loud clangs until it came to rest a couple of feet away from where Ben and Marty lay in a heap in front of the door.

They sat up quickly, wiping the places on their arms scraped by the concrete. Marty's elbow wound opened up and began to bleed a little again. As they were tending to their wounds, they looked up simultaneously in the direction of the house, fully expecting to hear someone coming towards them from inside the house. But instead they saw something that surprised them both.

The door was wide open.

Chapter Ten

"A love song must respect the canons of music beauty, entering the fibers of those who are listening." - Andrea Bocelli

Ben scrambled over to the side of the house where Marty had retreated and moved his body so it was flush with the brick. From his position below, Marty leaned over just enough to where he could glance into the door. He looked quickly inside and then sat back up against the house. He looked over at Ben and shrugged.

Ben realized the only weapon they had, the only chance they had of defending themselves should someone emerge from the house, was several feet away - directly in front of the open door. Standing against the house wasn't doing them any good. He quickly moved over and retrieved the crow bar, repositioning himself on the opposite side of the door where he started. He leaned over and looked into the dark house. Nothing was happening inside. No one moved toward the clamor and the open door. It was quiet, except for a faint sound coming from somewhere deeper inside the house. Ben motioned with his head and quickly slipped inside the door. Marty was surprised at the quick decision and it took him a few seconds to respond and get to his feet. *Thanks for the help up,* Marty thought. *It would be easier just to crawl. Probably safer, too - low man wins.*

Once Marty entered the house, he turned the flashlight on and moved it around. They were standing in an area with a small laundry room to the side, a half-bathroom behind a door, and then the hallway running through the center of the house. Starting with the laundry room and bathroom, they began checking the entire house. Marty was on flashlight, Ben on crowbar. They did their best to walk side-by-side down the hallway. It was a good thing breaking and entering was a deliberate process, because Marty only had one speed at the moment - slow. The first room they came to was on the left, and the door was closed. *Of course it is.*

Ben walked over to the door and quietly turned the handle, letting the door open slowly, carefully. When it was ajar enough to walk through, Marty shined the flashlight through the opening and Ben walked through, crowbar raised. Marty was right behind him, knowing this unwise adventure could go sideways at any moment - from the front or from behind. Just inside the doorway, Marty moved the beam of light all around the room. It was empty. Although as Marty pointed the light to the floor, there were furniture impressions in the carpet.

It hadn't been empty long.

Just to be safe, Ben went over to the closet and pulled the folding doors open to reveal a shallow space that was also empty.

Marty turned the flashlight back to the carpet and gestured to the furniture impressions, just to make sure Ben saw them. Ben nodded his head and they both retreated out of the first room, looking both ways down the hallway before moving back out into the corridor.

They repeated the same process in two other bedrooms, each empty and each containing fresh furniture impressions in the carpet. When they got to the room closest to the front of the house, they were finally able to determine the sound coming from the house was music. One song, to be specific, on replay. It was an operatic piece and it sounded like it was being sung in a foreign language. One neither Marty nor Ben recognized.

Upon leaving the third bedroom, they walked into a main room and looked around. There, they discovered the only piece of furniture left in the house. A dentist's chair sitting in the middle of the floor. Opposite the chair was a fireplace and resting upon the mantle was a battery-powered CD player, with music coming out from its speakers.

Marty moved closer to it and found himself in the middle of a moment of deja vu. "What song is this?" he asked out loud, before remembering he wasn't supposed to be making any noise. Hearing the song was like an old-time switchboard operator trying to plug Marty's present self directly into a moment in his past. Unfortuntately for Marty, the wire was connected, but there was nothing on the other line.

Ben was quickly at his side and whispered, "No idea. I've never heard it before."

~~~ ~~~ ~~~ ~~~ ~~~ ~~~ ~~~

"What song is this?" Marty asked, clearly not feeling it. They were sitting on a swing on Jane's back porch near dusk on a mild April evening. She was up under his shoulder, snuggled in close. He had one arm around her and a glass of tea in the other; they were talking, swinging and listening to a playlist Jane had put together.

"*Con te Partiro*. It's my favorite song in the whole world." Jane answered.

"Contay who?" Marty tried to joke, unsuccessfully.

"It's Italian, silly. It means "I'll go with you."

"That's nice, How can you listen to this? I can't understand a word he's saying."

"A song can still move you, even if you don't understand the words. He's singing about love, which is something you might know about?"

"Maybe."

"Alright, nerd. If you must know, this is what he's saying," and she began singing the English translation over the top of the Italian words of the chorus.

Time to say goodbye
to countries I never
saw and shared with you,
I shall experience them.
I'll go with you
on ships across seas
which, I know,
exist no longer.

"Isn't it beautiful?"

"You're beautiful."

"So you'll go with me? On ships across seas which exist no longer? Say you'll go with me."

"Whatever ship you're on, I'll be on. That you can be sure of."

Jane just smiled and sighed, placing her head on Marty's shoulder and continued to hum along to the rest of the music while crickets and frogs and other wild tiny things joined in the song.

It occurred to Marty that no one had ever sung to him before. Her voice was so angelic he wondered how

she could possibly be so good at everything she did. And how he was ever lucky enough to find her.

~~~ ~~~ ~~~ ~~~ ~~~ ~~~ ~~~

"Time to say goodbye." Ben said, speaking in a normal volume now. "Let's get out of here. I just checked the kitchen and front room and they're empty, too. Nobody's here. It's obvious the Professor has cleared out."

There was undeniable disappointment in his voice.

"Okay. But first let's see if there's anything I can use to help with my ankle," Marty said as he pushed stop on the CD, clicked the open button on the top and removed it from the player. He wasn't sure why he was taking it, and Ben's puzzled expression indicated he wasn't sure, either. But it had sparked something in Marty's mind and he felt it could be a clue to something at some point. So he put it on his right pinky finger and followed Ben out of the main room, briefly looking over his shoulder at the dentist chair again.

They moved into the kitchen area and began rummaging around.

Marty checked the refrigerator while Ben started opening up cabinets.

In the freezer, Marty found an ice pack which he pulled out and held up for Ben to see. Ben was holding something, too. A bottle of pain-reliever. "There are three pills left," he said.

They were the only two consumables in the entire house.

Marty took the three pills and swallowed them with his own saliva as they made their way back out the rear door.

"You sit here and put the ice on your ankle. I'll hoof it back through the woods, get the car, and come around to get you. Shouldn't take me more than twenty minutes to get back. I'll take the flashlight. You keep the crowbar."

"Alright. Be careful. There's some mean-spirited tree roots out there who would love to ruin your evening."

"Noted."

Ben took off in the direction of the woods and within moments Marty could see him disappear into the tree line.

Overhead, the sky began to rumble and Marty could see flashes of light off in the distance to the west.

"Storm's coming," Marty said out loud to no one in particular.

Then he laid his head back against the house and quickly fell asleep.

Chapter Eleven

"We do not remember days, we remember moments." - Cesare Pavese

Marty had the journal open on his lap and a pen in his right hand, carefully drawing lines through the bullet points, the once-cherished memories he no longer could recall. He eliminated six items before he finally reached one he could remember. He set the pen down and put both hands up to his face, rubbing his eyes, as if this activity might change the growing desperation of his current reality.

Ben watched Marty from the driver's seat as they sat in the parking lot of Marty's apartment complex in late afternoon. Seeing Marty cross off memory after memory must have been all too familiar to him. He reached over and squeezed Marty on the shoulder as if to say, "I know, man. I know." There would be no patronizing reassurances that everything would be ok. It hadn't turned out ok for Ben. The only thing either man could do was focus on the next step in the process.

"Is there anything you remember about the day you met the Professor? Anything he said? Did he mention something that might give us a clue as to where we can find him? Something. Anything. Just think." Ben said, with frustration in his voice.

"I can't think of anything. He said he was a professor of neuro-psy-something or other at a university in another part of the state."

"Ok, it's a large state, but there can't be *too* many colleges, can there? Let's check it out."

Ben pulled out a laptop computer from underneath the driver's seat.

"Do you have everything in this little car?" Marty asked, surprised and impressed all at the same time.

"Not everything. Thought about getting a shower installed, but it didn't seem practical."

Marty shook his head and laughed a little. *This guy.*

He handed the notebook to Marty who placed it in his lap, and they drove to a popular donut shop in the city. They walked in and found a booth close to the door. Ben clicked on the network, checked the appropriate boxes and soon they were connected to the internet. He typed in his search for colleges in the state into the search bar and instantly thousands of links came up. The first one was the official State University System website. Assuming it would be the most concise and official spot, he clicked on the link. There were several pages of schools listed, and by the time he clicked through them all, they both were a bit discouraged.

"By my count, there are thirty-two colleges and universities in the University System. Way too many to search each one. We have no name. All we know is his field. We could try to narrow the list down by that criteria. They can't all have neuroscience divisions."

"You wouldn't think so. It's a good place to start."

~~~ ~~~ ~~~ ~~~ ~~~ ~~~ ~~~

"It's as good a place to start as any," Jane said.

Marty was driving, Jane was shotgun, and Jane's sister, Joy was in the back seat. Marty and Jane were on a mission to find a unique wedding gift for Marty's sister, Mel, and Jane needed Joy to help pick out a dress for the occasion. As they were driving, brainstorming unusual places for the perfectly thoughtful present and appropriately elegant dress, Joy suggested an outdoor market/mall-hybrid located on the bank of a river north of the city.

It was a perfect day for outdoor strolling and shopping. The trio walked along, stopping when either of the girls saw something they wanted to investigate further, which was just about every shop or kiosk. Marty normally hated shopping, but this he didn't

mind so much. He was just happy to be there, holding Jane's hand.

They approached a vendor who had arrays of flowers set out for purchase in pots, vases, and plastic wrappers. Marty was just going to pass by it when he felt Jane tugging at his hand to stop.

She released his hand and began walking around the cart, looking at the arrangements, stooping to smell them, a look of wonder on her face, like an explorer who had just discovered rare treasure.

Marty glanced over at Joy, who remained near him instead of joining her sister.

"Jane loves flowers." Joy said.

"I've noticed." Marty replied.

"No, I'm not sure you understand. She *loves* them." Joy repeated, stretching out the word 'love' for emphasis. "Some of my first memories of her are her drawing flowers, picking flowers, wearing flowers in her hair like some child of the sixties."

"So she's a hippie, too? Everything makes so much more sense now." Marty said.

"I'm more Bohemian than Hippie. Although the lines of distinction are admittedly blurry." Jane said, finally looking up from the flowers with a bright smile on her face.

Jane finished her exploration and walked over to join the others.

"Which ones did you like the best, Bohemian woman?" Marty asked her.

"The peach roses. I just adore peach roses."

Jane and Joy saw a boutique they wanted to check out, and as soon as they disappeared inside, Marty doubled back to the flower stand.

When the girls emerged a few minutes later, Marty was standing outside the door of the shop with one hand behind his back, and a guilty look on his face.

"What are you up to?" Jane said, recognizing the look.

"Oh, nothing. Just standing here waiting on you two lovelies to wrap it up, already."

"Oh really? Well, if you're not up to anything, why do you have one arm behind your back?"

"I just like to stand this way. I find it comfortable."

Jane giggled and rushed to him, attempting to get behind him as Marty whirled around to keep the front of his body towards her. When she gave up, he extended his arm to reveal a single peach rose.

"You two are nauseating." Joy teased.

Jane laughed, took hold of the rose, and leaned up to kiss Marty on the cheek. As her lips retreated from his face, she moved them to his ear and said softly, "I love you more than flowers."

The hair on Marty's skin stood up as if he were about to be struck by lightning, goose bumps emerging underneath the hair. Inside, his soul was electrified with a current of emotion that was equal parts energizing and debilitating. He found it difficult to breathe normally. His knees were weak. He put his arm around her shoulder and pulled her close, partly because he wanted her as close as possible, and partly because if he didn't he might not be able to stand up.

He had never been told anything so beautiful in his whole life.

After shopping a couple of hours, they finally settled on a wedding gift. It was a personalized wooden wine box with three sliding compartments for three bottles of wine, the couple's last name in the center. Marty was planning on paying for all of it himself, after all it was his sister's wedding, but Jane insisted she wanted to be a part of the gift. Marty attempted to talk her out of it, but it was no use. When Jane set her mind to something, there was no convincing her otherwise, so Marty relented.

"It's settled then. We'll each pay half." Jane said, victorious.

Marty made eye contact with Joy, who had a *don't look at me, you know as well as I do how stubborn she is* expression.

Marty just shook his head, smiling.

～～～ ～～～ ～～～ ～～～ ～～～ ～～～ ～～～

"Let's divide this up sixteen and sixteen. You call half and I'll call half, each eliminating the schools without neuropsychiatry."

143

"That works. I'll take the first half," Marty said, as he began scribbling down numbers, one after the other into his journal. When he had written down all sixteen, he disappeared to find a booth of his own from which to make his calls. Ben was left with the laptop to get the last sixteen numbers.

Marty found a spot in the back corner, sat down, and dialed the first number on the list. It rang several times before an automated message came on. "Thank you for calling Aberdeen College, our regular office hours are Monday-Friday, 8 a.m. to 5 p.m. To hear a list of choices, press star now. Otherwise, you may hang up and try again during normal business hours. Thank you." Marty clicked the end button on his cell phone and checked the time. It was 6:15 p.m. And it was Friday. It was his first awareness of day and time in quite a while, and with it was the sudden realization - they wouldn't be able to find anything out until Monday morning, postponing the search for two and a half days.

Two days when he only had eight to twelve left, maybe less.

He rose from his seat and made his way back over to the table where Ben was sitting. He was just getting to the voice mailbox of the first college he called. The same realization hit him as he looked at his watch and then to Marty as he walked up. He ended the call and set the phone down on the table. "Friday night," he said, verbalizing the angst they both felt.

Marty sat down opposite Ben, neither of them saying anything. Ben closed the computer and set it aside, while Marty ran his hands nervously, slowly across the table. Eventually, he opened up his journal to the Memory List. His eyes made their way down to the bottom of the list. Grabbing the pen, he started scratching through another memory. "How many?" Ben asked. "Eight now," Marty responded, and scratched out another entry on the list. As he closed the journal, his elbow knocked the pen cap somewhere onto the booth behind where he was sitting. He reached down to retrieve it and noticed a card lodged halfway between the back of the bench and the seat.

Marty put his fingers on the card, tugging it gently, but so as not to dislodge it. He didn't want to retrieve it, he was reliving something. This was a familiar experience. He had done something similar recently. From across the table, Ben noticed the puzzled look on Marty's face. "What is it?" he asked, and ducked to look under the table at whatever Marty was pre-occupied with. "That's it!" Marty said suddenly, startling Ben so much that he bumped his head on the table while sitting back up. Marty jumped out of the seat and said, "Come on, we've got to go!" Ben, rubbing his head, said, "I'm okay, thanks for asking."

"I'm sorry, but I just remembered something about the day I met the Professor. We've got to go, I'll explain on the way."

Sensing the urgency, and perhaps a bit of hope, Ben said no more and followed Marty out the door. They crossed the street and Ben fumbled with his keys, dropping them on the ground and swearing under his breath. He picked them up, unlocked the driver's door, and slid down into his seat. He reached over and pulled up the lock on the passenger door. Marty got in and said, "drive to the bus stop where you found me," as he was shutting the door.

"Ok. What's going on?"

"I saw a business card stuck in the booth seat at the donut shop and it triggered my memory. The Professor gave me a business card on the day we met."

"He did what?"

"I know. I can't believe I didn't think of this before. He handed it to me as I sat in the rain. I wasn't really interested in talking to him at the time and so I stuffed it down between the slats on the bench. It's a long shot, but I think there's a chance it might still be there. It's definitely worth a look."

"This could be huge," Ben said, stating the obvious.

"I know. But it might not be there. And even if it is, the elements have had several days to go to work on it. It might have blown away or been washed out by the rain. But maybe, just maybe…" Marty let the thought trail off as they both thought about the implications of those maybes.

"Do you remember anything written on the card?"

"I didn't even look at it. Like I said, I didn't really care at the time. All I wanted was for this stranger to leave me alone and go away so I could continue sulking, over whatever it was I was sulking over. Man, I wish I had just glanced at it."

"Can't change the past, my friend. All we can do is shape the future. Let's find that card, track down the Professor, and get your memory back." Ben said, feeling invigorated by this new bit of fortune.

In less than ten minutes, Ben pulled up opposite the bus stop and parked in the same spot he had just a few days earlier when Marty woke up on the bench in his hospital gown.

"Talk about deja vu," Ben tried to joke.

"Yep, all I need is a splitting headache, wild hair, and a hospital gown," Marty answered, loosening some.

"I thought you wore the gown well. It looked good on you."

Marty laughed and said, "Thanks, I might buy a couple when this is all over."

They exited the vehicle, and quickly jogged to the intersection. When the light turned, they crossed and headed over to the bus stop. Just being back there for the first time gave Marty a very uneasy feeling. But perhaps the place where he was at his lowest point could be the place that started him on the journey toward healing. Maybe that's the way it always was supposed to work, *has* to work.

They reached the bus stop and saw two people were sitting there. One was a man in his seventies and the other a middle-aged woman, talking loudly on her cell phone. The old man next to her was clearly annoyed with this and kept looking over at her with a disapproving glare. She ignored his obvious body language and continued her conversation unabated. Marty noted she was sitting directly above the slats he pushed the business card down through. They would have to wait until she left.

Ben and Marty tried to act casual. They were just friends waiting for a bus. They talked about the weather for a minute or two and then let the conversation fade into awkward silence as the woman continued to jabber on into her cell phone. They stood about four feet behind the bench. Far enough away to be casual, and close enough to pounce as soon as the lady caught her bus. They took turns staring at their phones, glancing at each other with *will she ever leave* faces, and watching for buses.

Finally, the woman stood, and Ben and Marty tensed up. *Here we go*, they both thought and subconsciously moved closer to the bench. The lady stepped about two feet in front of the bench, and suddenly her voice became quiet, like she was whispering something into the cell phone she didn't want the audience she was previously regaling to hear. In about forty-five seconds, she backed up and sat right back down where she was. The old man rolled his eyes and shook his head. Marty gritted his teeth and Ben made a strangling gesture with his hands, to which Marty shot him a *cut it out* look.

Soon, cell phone lady ended her call, placed her phone in her purse, and pulled out a gossip magazine and started reading. The old man relaxed in his spot and mumbled something under his breath. Marty guessed it was something along the lines of "It's about time." It wasn't two minutes later the number 58 bus pulled up and the old man gingerly rose from his seat and waddled over and onto the bus. The poor guy only had a couple of minutes of silence to enjoy before he had to go.

Unfortunately for Ben and Marty, this wasn't the woman's bus. To make matters worse, her cell phone rang. She answered it and began her loud conversation all over again. Ben moved around and sat where the old man had been sitting. The lady looked him up and down as he sat down. She was clearly pleased with his appearance and irritated by his presence, all at the same time. Ben smiled and nodded at her, trying to be pleasant. She faked a smile back at him, then continued her conversation as if he weren't even there.

This went on for another fifteen minutes until the woman's bus finally arrived. She got up ceremoniously, never breaking her conversation or lowering her volume as she stepped onto the bus.

Marty swung around the bench and sat where she had just left.

"There's nothing worse than a warm seat," he said to Ben.

"Especially a large one," Ben said back.

Looking around to see if anyone was watching, Marty turned around and got on his knees in front of the bench, his hand probing in between the wooden slats. "If I remember correctly, and if we're incredibly fortunate, the card should be right…around…this…spot." In just a matter of seconds, Marty pulled a rectangular piece of paper previously stuck to an old piece of gum out from between the bench spaces and held it up for Ben and him to inspect.

"Is that the card?" Ben asked, hopeful.

"I'm pretty sure. Some of it is obscured by the gum and by the elements it's been exposed to. But, somehow, it was still here. I think this is a good sign."

Marty held it up and examined it while Ben slid down the bench to get a closer look. Realizing how strange they must look, Marty hopped up and sat on the bench next to Ben so they could look at it at the same time. It was pretty badly damaged from being outside for a few days. Dirt and pink gum were covering up some of the vital information.

With Marty picking the gum off little by little and wiping it beneath the wood on the bench, they could begin to make out parts of an address.

L e Uni ers ty, 619 W ll ks St et

Chapter Twelve

"The beauty of a woman must be seen from in her eyes, because that is the doorway to her heart, the place where love resides." - Audrey Hepburn

Slow down, man.

Trying to catch up with Ben, who had made it across before the light turned green, Marty rushed across the street as soon as the walk signal came up. Looking up ahead to spot his friend, he didn't see the person in front of him drop her bag as she stepped up on the curb. She bent down to pick it up and Marty walked right into her, pushing her forward onto her hands as he stumbled a few steps before catching himself. He immediately turned around to see what had happened. When he noticed the girl picking herself and her bag back up off the ground, he was mortified and rushed over to help her.

"I'm so sor…" As she stood up and they made eye contact, something pierced Marty deep in his core. It startled him so much he couldn't finish what he was saying.

To his bewilderment, the girl looked as if she recognized him.

Then she said his name.

"Marty! What are you doing here?"

"I'm so sorry I knocked you down. And I'm even more sorry to say this, but, do we know each other?"

"You didn't knock me down. It was my fault. I dropped my bag and I stopped suddenly to pick it up. There's was no way you could have anticipated that. And stop playing around. Of course we know each other. So crazy to run into you here. I mean, you actually ran into me, but what are you doing here?"

"I'm sorry. I know this sounds crazy, but I've been having some issues with my memory lately, and I honestly don't know who you are. How do we know each other?"

"Marty come on. I'm Joy……Jane's sister. Stop messing around."

He was thinking of what he could say next when he heard Ben calling his name. He was jogging back to get Marty.

"You've got to come with me. Now."

"Alright, I'm coming," Marty answered.

Looking back at the strange girl with the familiar eyes, he said, "Again, I'm so sorry, You seem like a really nice person. But I just don't have time to figure this out right now. Maybe we'll run into each other again sometime and we can sort this out." As he was finishing his sentence he was already walking backward in the direction Ben was going. As soon as he was done talking, he turned around quickly and started chasing after Ben, who was already up to the next intersection.

"Just another couple of blocks." Ben said.

As Marty followed along, he tried to make sense of the encounter he had just experienced. Those eyes. Looking into them had done something inside him. But why? Who was Joy? Whoever she was, someone named Jane was apparently the person who connected them. Could Jane be her? The person he had asked the Professor to erase from his memory? *Unlikely. Of all the people in the world, what are the chances a complete stranger would mention her. What if it wasn't even a "her"? It could have just as easily been a "him".* Perhaps both. Still, maybe he should have convinced Ben to stay and talk. Perhaps they could have uncovered more of the mystery. Maybe Joy was important in this whole thing. *Nobody is as important as the Professor*, Marty reminded himself. If they didn't stay hot on his trail, they might not find him in time for it to matter. Marty had already crossed out two more items on the memory list when he woke up this morning. Things he remembered yesterday, but were now gone, maybe forever.

Whoever Joy was, whatever reason her eyes resonated with Marty so deeply, would have to wait. Marty was determined to find the Professor before it was too late. He had to. But those eyes.

~~~ ~~~ ~~~ ~~~ ~~~ ~~~ ~~~

They were in a canoe, and Marty was paddling down the river. Oar in the water on one side, then the other. Repeat. They had been canoeing for about an hour. Marty was doing all of the work, and he was perfectly okay with it. It was a one-person canoe, really. Jane sat in front of Marty, between his legs, pointing out things she thought were interesting or beautiful, reaching into the cooler and getting a soda when either of them needed another. He pretended to

be interested in what she would point out, and under any other circumstance, he probably would have been. But all he could seem to focus on was the way her brunette pony tail would sway as she looked back and forth or how her thin, tan shoulders looked on either side of and beneath the spaghetti straps of her bathing suit top.

It was a mild early spring day, with the requisite forty percent chance of rain. And, sure enough, there were a few thunderclouds flanking the river on the eastern side. But so far, it had stayed dry. A discussion about nothing in particular had become something more without much effort. It's funny how mundane things can escalate into something electric when two hearts want them to. Jane had teased Marty by saying she loved the sun so much she was going to try to stare at it for a few seconds. Just a few seconds wouldn't hurt a thing. And she looked up in the direction of the sun as if she were looking right at it.

Marty reached up with his free hand and gently pushed her head down while saying "Quit it. You'll burn your eyes and then you won't be able to see my ruggedly-handsome face anymore."

She giggled and leaned back into him, pretending to shake his hand off her head.

Trying to sound wise and bait Jane into a bet at the same time, Marty repeated something he had heard one of his mentors say many years ago.

"You know you can't stare into another person's eyes without something dangerous happening, either."

"Hmm. Sounds like you made that up, mister."

"Nope. It's a proven psychological fact."

"Oh *really*?"

"Really. If two people stare into each other's eyes, within sixty seconds they will be either kissing or fighting."

Never one to back down from a challenge, Jane turned her head around so she was looking directly into Marty's eyes and started counting down from sixty. *It worked!* With each second she counted, their lips moved closer and closer together. She didn't make it past fifty.

Marty leaned in slowly and kissed her mouth. It was soft and warm and true. A million roman candles went up inside his heart, his life suddenly brighter and more colorful than it had ever been before. There's something different about a first kiss. Its power is singular. In relationships, people forget thousands - maybe tens of thousands - of kisses along the way. But they never forget the first. It's a beacon, calling them back to the innocent and the pure, when love was young, when love was new. Marty withdrew his lips just a fraction of a centimeter and could feel a smile breaking out across Jane's lips. He opened his eyes to get a glimpse of her face. Her eyes were still closed.

"More" was all she said, in almost a whisper. "More."

~~~ ~~~ ~~~ ~~~ ~~~ ~~~ ~~~

"One more. Should be just one more block. Yep, it's up there. That building on the right after the one covered in ivy. 619 Willcocks Street. We're on Willcocks and there is building 619. That's where his office is, assuming the process of elimination we went through yielded the correct address."

A big if, Marty thought. Things had been difficult, to say the least. No reason to assume they would start going smoothly now. Marty was a bit of a pessimist by nature, anyway. He would say he was a "realist," and there was an element of truth to that. But those closest to him knew in any given situation his inclination was to assume the worst rather than the best. This was a source of tension for Marty, who prided himself on being self-aware. But it's hard for people to change who they are.

Outside of 619 Willcocks Street was a sign reading *Department of Behavioral Neurology and Neuropsychiatry.* Ben pointed to it and then flashed a smile and a thumbs up sign. Maybe their luck was turning. This had to be the place listed on the Professor's business card. Marty pumped his fist in response to the thumbs up and they made their way to the front of the building. It was faded white with four large columns, looking as if it could have been plopped down on any campus in America and fit right in. Ben, with Marty right behind him, hopped up onto the first step and they quickly made their way up to the massive wood doors leading into the building. With a sigh, Ben placed his hand on the substantial door handle and gave it a tug.

It wouldn't open.

Ben and Marty looked at each other as if to say, "figures." It was Saturday morning after all and therefore unreasonable to expect the building to be open. Ben sat down on the top step and soon Marty followed suit. They sat there for a while, taking in the activity on the Quad in front of them. Marty took particular notice of the girls walking by. Ben did, too, but he pretended not to notice. After all, he was a little bit too old to be interested in college girls. Although, no doubt, they'd still be interested in him. His strong jawline, youthful face, and piercing green eyes were enough to get any woman's attention. The rugged appearance his beard gave him didn't hurt, either. As Ben sat there, he wondered what his late teens and early twenties must have been like. The girls he knew, the experiences he had, the lessons he learned. He would never know. All he had were a few lines written down in a journal. Those experiences might as well have happened to somebody else. To him they were just words on a page.

Marty made eye contact with an extremely attractive red-head. The connection made him blush and he quickly turned away. When he looked up her back was to him, walking with friends down the street. The sudden eye contact reminded him of what he experienced just a few minutes earlier. He could still see those eyes. He tried to remember what the rest of her face looked like, but all he could see were the eyes. He wasn't sure if he had ever seen anything more stunning. And now that they were just sitting and waiting outside the building, he really wished he had taken the time to talk to her more. She *knew* him. And he didn't know her. There could only be two explanations for this. Either she was a part of his earlier life, the part he was already starting to forget. Or his only connection to her was the person he had removed from his memory.

Jane. That had to be it. If he had known her earlier in life, surely she wouldn't recognize him now.

He pulled his journal out from the back of his waist and opened it to the memory list. He scanned down to the oldest memories that hadn't been scratched off yet. There was one more he couldn't recall, and made a mental note to eliminate it as soon as he had a pen. But there were still memories from his early teen years in play. If this mystery girl were part of his early lost memories, she would have known him before he became a teenager. It just didn't make sense that she would so easily recognize him now. She had to be a connection to the person the Professor erased from his mind. And he had left her. Left her to continue this wild goose chase with the Bearded Wonder.

"Ben, there's something I think you should know," Marty said.

Despite his best efforts not to notice, Ben had been staring at a group of girls gathered across the street. He was so startled when Marty broke the silence he started looking around to try to play it off.

"What is it?" Ben said, finally.

"Well, when you came back to get me on the corner about thirty minutes ago…"

Marty's revelation was interrupted by the sound of the heavy door opening behind them. It made a slow and hollow creak in cadence with the click of hard-soled shoes on the marble floor behind it. They both held their breath and turned around casually, hoping against hope it was the Professor walking out.

Disappointment.

It was a woman of Asian descent in a sharp business suit, a briefcase in her left hand and a cup of coffee in the other. She walked straight toward them and they had to move to make a path for her to walk down the stairs. "Excuse us," Ben said. A comment which she ignored as she made her way down the steps. The fact she paid no attention to the them was actually a relief to both of the men. No questions about who they were or why they were there. In a matter of moments she turned down the street. They watched her until she was out of eyesight.

Marty was the first to turn back toward the door.

It wasn't closed all the way.

Chapter Thirteen

"A dead end street is a good place to turn around."
- Naomi Judd

"Ben!" Marty said with excitement in his voice. Ben turned around and noticed what Marty had seen. He jumped to his feet and quickly walked over to the door. He looked around, and then gave the long handle a quick tug. The door came open slightly.

They were in.

It was the second time a door had unexplainably, perhaps magically, opened for them.

Ben looked around furtively while Marty watched his face for a signal. There were plenty of people in the general area, but none of them cared about what was going on at the top of the steps of an academic office building. Ben gave an *everything's good* look and slid sideways through the door. Marty, thinking it was a bit ridiculous, opened the door enough for him to walk through while shaking his head and rolling his eyes at Ben's overdramatic entrance.

Inside, the building appeared empty. There was a hollow feeling to it, and the only light was the sunlight coming in from windows at the top of the structure, casting eerie shadows across the floor. The ground floor was an open room with high ceilings. In the middle of the floor were twin staircases curving opposite each other up to a second floor surrounding the perimeter of the inside of the building.

The first thing Marty noticed was the smell. It invaded his senses. He felt his stomach catch and moisture begin to form at the corners of his eyes. And he had no idea why.

~~~ ~~~ ~~~ ~~~ ~~~ ~~~ ~~~

"This place smells funny," Jane said, eyes covered with a blindfold, giggling with nervous laughter. "Where are we? And are we even *supposed* to be in here?"

"Of course we're *supposed* to be. It's not open to the general public right now, but I have connections."

"Oh, you have *connections,* huh? Well aren't you something."

"Well, I have lots of connections. But this one particular connection is a very, um, important man." Marty was having trouble finishing his sentence because Jane was looking in his direction with a sarcastic smile, raising her eyebrows further with every phrase in mock anticipation.

"I see. So this very important man, he just let us in here?"

"Actually, if I'm being honest, I don't really know anyone important. I called last week and asked if I could rent it out for a couple of hours." Marty said, admitting defeat.

Jane just started laughing and the sound bounced off the old walls of the building.

"It's got a funny smell to it, but I like the way our voices sound when they echo. When are you going to tell me where we are and what we're doing here? What's so important you had to call upon your *connections* to make this happen?" she teased.

"Come with me," Marty said, grabbing her hand as he began to walk through the quiet halls of the on-campus Art Museum.

"Well, where else would I go? I can't see anything."

He led her down a long corridor until they suddenly turned left into an open room with paintings covering the walls. It was the only room in the building with the lights on. Marty scanned the walls until his eyes found what he was looking for. *There it is,* the excitement in his stomach crescendoing.

Jane, sensing the brightness in the room through the blindfold, said "Did you set the place on fire?"

"Not exactly."

He led her over and positioned her in front of the east wall, about halfway down.

"Okay, I'm going to take the blindfold off now."

"Finally!"

166

Marty walked behind Jane and slowly, deliberately, dramatically began to undo the cloth covering her eyes. He let it fall to the floor below her feet and waited for the reaction he hoped would be overwhelming.

In front of Jane's eyes, hanging alongside significant art from many great painters, was one of her own pieces of art. It was the picture of an old white house with a wrap-around porch, porch swing in the corner, chipped paint, tall grass growing up all around it, one window shutter sitting askew by the front window, a little girl on the front step, a single rose in one hand, the other hand holding the key, refusing to go inside. Jane had painted it in high school as a way of coping with the loss of her father. He had been gone ten years when she created this. Ten years since he called to say he would be home in five minutes and was never heard from again. The white house embodied the idealism and memory of her childhood. The little girl was Jane herself frozen in time. She was holding the key to healing, wanting so badly to go in, but unable to move.

Jane stood there, in front of her own work, and the tears began to fall. Her knees became weak and she collapsed gently onto the side of her legs and rear end, Marty reaching down in an attempt to catch her. She grabbed the bandana that had served as her blindfold and used it to wipe away some of the tears now flowing in waves down her face.

Marty had begun to think he had made a terrible mistake until he heard Jane softly say, "Thank you. Thank you so much." Her words trailed off at the end and Marty sat down behind her. She leaned against him and shook with emotion. He wrapped his arms around her and they sat there on the floor of the museum for a long time. She later told him it was in that moment she realized she never wanted to be with anyone else.

~~~ ~~~ ~~~ ~~~ ~~~ ~~~ ~~~

"You know, since the day I saw you stalking me from across the street, I keep getting these weird Deja vu feelings. It doesn't happen when I'm around anyone else." Marty said softly.

"I do seem to bring out the electric impulses in your brain," Ben whispered back, playing along. "What was it this time?"

"I don't know. I think it's the smell of this place."

The two walked the ground floor to the base of the stairs, creeping along, trying to make as little noise as possible. They hoped the building was empty, but they had already seen one person leave. It was possible others were working as well. Ben was in front and chose the staircase on the left to begin his ascent to the second floor. Marty took the one on the right.

When they reached the top, Ben looked over at Marty from the top of the other staircase and held up his phone to indicate he would be sending Marty something. Marty saw Ben begin to type a text message. In just a few seconds or so, his phone lit up.

"Let's split up. I'll go this way and you go right. Check all the doors. Look for any pictures or names outside offices. Anything Middle-Eastern should be explored further, if possible. Also, we need to stop sneaking around. Let's act like we're supposed to be here. Any news report back."

Marty looked over at Ben and nodded his agreement.

After about thirty minutes, the two were back where they started at the top of the stairs. Not a single unlocked door. No clues. No unusual names. Everything was Smith and Brown and Jones and Chang. All Drs. of course.

"I can't believe we came all this way for nothing." Marty said as they descended the staircase together on the same side.

"Hey!" A voice called from down below. Marty and Ben were both obviously startled.

They looked down to see a woman standing between the two staircases. It was the same woman they saw leaving the building earlier.

Busted.

"Can I help you? You're not supposed to be in here."

Ben spoke first. "We were, we were looking for our neuropsychiatry professor." He lied.

"Oh. Well what is his name?"

Nice going, genius.

"We don't…actually know his name."

"You don't know your Professor's name? Not even his last name?"

The two men just stood there.

"May I see your student I.D.'s please?" the lady asked.

"We left them back at our dorm…" Ben started to fib again, but the lady, eyebrows raised and arms folded, wasn't buying it, so Marty interrupted.

"Actually, ma'am, we don't go to school here…

"We were looking for someone I met the other day. Someone we thought could help us with a problem we are having. He offered to assist us and he gave us his business card. We used the information on the card to track him here."

"Well if you have his business card, how is it possible you don't know his name?"

Fair question. But one impossible to answer without sounding crazy. Marty and Ben looked at each other before Marty responded vaguely, "It's a long story."

"I don't have time for long stories today. Nor do I have time for young men who are not even students of this university snooping around these offices. I'm going to ask you to leave. If you refuse to leave, I will call campus security and they will escort you off the premises."

"Yes ma'am. We'll leave." Marty agreed, the dejection and frustration evident in his tone. What seemed like a huge break, a clue leading somewhere promising, a sign of progress, turned out to be one gigantic and disappointing dead end. The lady followed them out and as soon as they walked out the door, she slammed the large wooden doors behind them, tugging against them to make sure they were shut for good. The sound of the slam jolted both Marty and Ben, not just physically, but emotionally as well. They had been kicked out, jettisoned, exiled from their quest to find the Professor. With no new clues and nothing to go on, they had to admit to themselves and each other they had lost the scent.

"What are we going to do now?" Marty said, thinking aloud.

"I don't know," Ben answered, a lot quicker than Marty would have liked. It sounded a lot like defeat, like a surrender.

Ben started to walk down the steps and out onto the sidewalk, leaving Marty behind.

"Hey! Where are you going?"

"Somewhere where I can get a stiff drink." Ben called over his shoulder.

"Do you want me to come with you?" Marty, shouting now.

Ben stopped and turned back for a second. "I'll be in touch,' was all he said before heading down the street alone.

When Marty made it back to his apartment, he collapsed onto the couch. It had been another long day. He opened his memory list and went down to the first item not scratched off. And he couldn't remember it. He went up three more bullet points before he got to a memory he still retained. The clock was ticking and they were no closer to finding the Professor than they had been when they started. In fact, the trail had gone cold.

Ice cold.

Marty lay on the couch, staring up at the ceiling, wondering if he would ever hear from Ben again, if they would ever find the Professor, if he would ever remember.

Chapter Fourteen

"Sometimes, you feel like you've sold your soul. But if I win the lottery, I'm going to buy it back." - Mark Addy

The next morning, Marty woke up with a start, sitting straight up on the couch. The dream. It was the girl he saw yesterday. Or was it? It looked like her, but not exactly like her. Same eyes, same mouth, same color hair. No, it wasn't her. It was someone else. Maybe a relative?

What was the dream? Marty concentrated really hard for a few moments. Grasping at the remnants of it, trying not to let it slip away into oblivion. Oh. Yes. It was the two of them, whoever she was. They were at a gas station filling a white SUV up with gas.

~~~ ~~~ ~~~ ~~~ ~~~ ~~~ ~~~

"Have you ever played the lottery?" Jane asked Marty.

"A couple of times. Never won anything. You?"

"I've played the jackpot before, but I've never bought a scratch off. Will you buy me a scratch-off?"

"I'll buy you as many scratch-offs as you want."

"Well, then I want five. Five scratch-offs, Marty McFly." Jane said, referencing the movie *Back to the Future*, which they had watched together only a few nights before.

"Five scratch-offs? What if they say no? I just don't think I can handle that kind of rejection." Marty said, playing along.

"Five scratch-offs. Please. And I guarantee no rejection on this side of things."

"Okay, I'll be right back." Marty said, as he placed the pump back in its cradle and walked inside to get them.

He returned in just a few moments, opened the driver's side door and climbed up into the seat. He presented the tickets to Jane as if they were something for which he had been looking for a long time, and couldn't wait to share his discovery. "You'll never guess what I found inside."

"Hand 'em over!" Jane said with an excitement disproportionate to the likely result of scratching off a lottery ticket. Chances were, they weren't going to win anything.

"Here you go. Win us some money."

"I plan to. But let's make it a little more interesting, shall we?" Jane was talking in such a way that Marty knew they were on the verge of her launching them into an adventure.

He was right.

"If we win anything, anything at all, money, a ticket, whatever, we take our winning ticket to a gas station in the next town, turn it in for however many new tickets we can get with what we've won. We repeat the process until we either run out of money, or win at least twenty dollars. The only stipulation is we don't spend any more money than we have already spent. What do you say?"

"Sounds good to me. You want to do the first one?" Marty said, reaching down to grab a coin from the console of the car. Jane scratched off each box as if she was opening a present at a birthday party. Very deliberate, savoring the excitement.

"Would you hurry up already? At this rate we won't ever leave the gas station."

"Okay, okay. Calm yourself, mister." Jane responded, hurriedly unveiling all of the numbers. It wasn't a winner.

Marty got the next one with the same result. Back and forth they went until all five were completely scratched off, little silver shavings all over the seats and console of the vehicle.

They were 0 for 5.

"Well, so much for that idea," Marty said.

"You give up too easy. Five more?" Jane said, her eyes big, head nodding as if there was no other choice.

"We don't spend any more money. That was your *only* rule!" Marty laughed, knowing it would make no difference, and not really caring to abide by the rules anyway.

He continued to laugh, shook his head, and went back in to the convenience store. He emerged in a couple of minutes with ten more tickets. "A little insurance to make sure we at least get out of the gate." He explained. This time they split the tickets and both went to work furiously scratching. Even as Marty was striking out on his third ticket, Jane shrieked on ticket number two. "I think I won!"

"Let me see! How much?" Marty said almost at the same time.

She handed the winning ticket over to him excitedly and he confirmed her discovery. They had won three dollars.

"It's a winner. Three bucks! Well done, baby."

And off they went to a convenience store the next town over. They bought three tickets there. Every single one was a winner.

At the next stop, even further from home, their journey nearly came to an end. They were down to their last scratch on their last ticket before they hit a six dollar winner. The intrigue came to an end a couple of gas stations later, not with the better scenario of winning twenty dollars or more, but by eventually purchasing four tickets that were all losers. Overall, they made it to seven different convenience stores in seven different towns, making it nearly to the state line, over one hundred miles from where they started.

"Take me to the shore." Jane said, after the last ticket came up empty. "Take me to the shore, babe." She had her eyes closed and she was leaning over to put her head on his shoulder. It was dusk and she was feeling sleepy.

"We should get back. It's over a two-hour ride back home."

"I don't want to go back home right now. Take me to the shore."

"Why do you want to go to the shore, silly girl?"

Jane spoke as if she was imagining a scene in her mind already, her tone wistful and dreamy: "I want to lay with you in the sand and listen to the sound of the waves gently slap the shore. I want to hear you talk sweetly in my ear. I want to look out on the water and imagine ships taking us across seas which no longer exist. Will you go with me?"

Marty's heart was enlarging with each sentence. It was beating so wildly for this girl it felt like it would detach from its moorings and roam freely inside his chest. Her words were always the most beautiful words. And if there was anything he loved, anything he needed most, it was beautiful words.

He had always been good with words. Always felt he could find a way to say just the right thing. He sometimes wondered if people had not fallen for him so much as they had fallen for his words. And he had always been disappointed nobody else could return the words he had sent out back to his heart. Until he met Jane. She had the words. The words inflated his hope, relieved tension he never even consciously felt, unlocked a million different doors to his soul.

They stopped at a superstore and purchased a flashlight, double sleeping bag, paper cups, a bottle of red wine and Little Debbie Nutty Bars. He drove her the thirty or so miles to get to the shore of the large lake that created part of the state border. They crawled up under the sleeping bag, drank red wine out of plastic cups and finished off the box of Nutty Bars. They marveled at what seemed like trillions of stars forming a canopy over their heads. Marty pointed out constellations to Jane - The Big Dipper, Orion, Cassiopeia. She mentioned something she had read on the internet recently.

"You know, they say all of the atoms in our bodies used to be a part of a star. I like to think about some primitive couple laying on the grass one night long ago, looking up, and wishing on you and me."

"We're made of stars..." Marty said, wonder in his tone.

As they lay back looking up at the night sky, Marty whispered things in her ear. Things he wanted her to

know. Things he'd never told anyone before. The whispers turned into an embrace, and the embrace turned into passionate kissing. This went on for over an hour before Jane lowered her head and rested it on Marty's chest, her head moving up and down with the wild beating of his heart. And they both drifted off, rocked to sleep by the sound of the waves slowly crawling up the shore.

And they slept until they were awoken by the rising sun.

~~~ ~~~ ~~~ ~~~ ~~~ ~~~ ~~~

The rising sun was beginning to penetrate the windows. And Marty's conscious mind was still in an SUV at a gas station with a girl he didn't recognize.

Try as he might, Marty couldn't recall any more of the dream. It frustrated him because he felt it might be a clue, a shadow of the person he tried to forget. And it gave him hope that if he saw this person in his dream, then maybe she was still in there, somewhere. He had read once that the people we don't recognize in our dreams are not fabrications, but those we've met before and just don't remember. Recalling his memory tutorial with Ben, he guessed the hippocampus had decided to file those kinds of people somewhere other than the conscious mind. But they were there. And so she must be there. Unless he was crazy and he was just dreaming about the girl he ran into yesterday. The girl with the eyes he couldn't forget.

He needed fresh air, needed to clear his head. He grabbed his keys and, without bothering to change clothes or even brush his teeth or hair, he left the apartment. He needed coffee for sure, but he also had an inexplicable desire to buy lottery tickets. So he biked up to the closest gas station. He filled up a cup with the gas station's coffee and sipped it. *Not terrible.* He made his way to the counter and asked the attendant for five $2 scratch-offs.

While he was waiting for the man to return with the tickets, his eyes wandered and caught sight of a display with different types of puzzle books. Word Search, Sudoku, and one crossword puzzle book. On its cover, it said "Crossword Puzzles are known to help increase alertness, vocabulary, and in some cases sharpen intellect and memory." *Sharpen memory? I'm pretty good at crosswords. Quite good, actually. And I'm desperate enough to try anything at this point.*

He took a few steps over to the rack, removed the crossword puzzle book, and set it on the counter. "This, too." he said to the man, who had finally returned with the lottery tickets. Marty paid the man, received his change, and walked outside. He sat down on the curb next to his bike, set the crossword puzzle book on the ground beside him, and sipped the black coffee while he scratched off five non-winning lottery tickets.

Stupid lottery never got anyone anywhere.

Chapter Fifteen

"Everything that happens once can never happen again. But everything that happens twice will surely happen a third time." - Paulo Coelho

Marty finished the last few sips of his coffee, even though it had become lukewarm.

He folded the crossword puzzle book and placed it in his back pocket, threw the coffee cup in the recycling bin, and climbed on his bike. It was a chilly morning, but not too cold, almost perfect for a bike ride around the city. He didn't have anywhere in particular to be, so he headed out toward a park near school. He rode along with the memory journal tucked between his skin and waistline and the puzzle book which was slowly creeping its way out of his back pocket. About halfway to the park, it slipped free of the confines of Marty's jeans and fell to the ground.

Marty reached the park and rolled his bike up to one of the benches. He was about to lock it and sit down when he realized what was missing from his pocket. Aggravated with himself, or with the difficulty of life, or both, he hopped back on his bike and re-traced the path he had just taken, keeping his eyes open for the book. He didn't know why it was so important that he go to all of this trouble to retrieve it. It only cost him $3.99 plus tax, so it wasn't the money. He just felt like there was a reason he bought it. There had to be some reason he went to the gas station that morning, and the lottery tickets certainly weren't the answer.

A couple of miles back, Marty saw the puzzle book laying undisturbed on the sidewalk. As he coasted in to retrieve it, he saw a male pedestrian close in, reach down, and grab the puzzle book.

"Hey!" Marty called out, not in an angry tone, but a positive, get-your-attention tone. The man turned to look at Marty as he alit from his bike and started pushing it down the sidewalk toward him. "That's my puzzle book. I dropped it on my way to the park and when I got there and realized I had lost it I immediately turned around to come get it."

"It was just laying here. And I found it. You can't prove it's yours." The man sounded juvenile and Marty realized he wasn't all there mentally.

"I can prove it. There's an orange sticker on the top right corner that has the price. It says $3.99."

"Lucky guess," the man responded.

So that's how you're going to be, huh?

"Please give me my book back. It's not worth much at all. Please."

"It's worth four dollars, the way I see it."

186

Oh, so you're turning this into a money grab. Okay. Whatever.

Marty looked into his pocket and pulled out three one-dollar bills. "This is all the cash I have on me. Honest. Three bucks. What do you say?"

The man walked over to Marty and eyed the three bills in his outstretched hand. "Oh, alright. Here you go."

Marty handed over the money and the man gave Marty his crossword puzzle book back. "No pleasure doing business with you." Marty muttered under his breath as he turned his bike around, hopped on it, and began to pedal away. He looked at the book in his left hand. *I bought you twice in a matter of two hours. You better be worth it.*

~~~ ~~~ ~~~ ~~~ ~~~ ~~~ ~~~

This better be worth it. Marty thought.

He and Jane were attending a lecture she insisted would be great for both of them. The topic advertised was "Inner Strength" and professed to help listeners find power from within, even during difficult or stressful times. The speaker was a tall, thin man in his late-forties. He was wearing khakis and a sport jacket

and reminded Marty of an uncle he hadn't seen in years. The event was sponsored by a campus student organization and was held in an old house that had been re-purposed for student gatherings. Most of the building had been updated, at least to a degree; everything but the old tin roof.

After about ten minutes, Marty had heard enough. He didn't have much patience for people who liked to hear themselves talk, or for pre-packaged, one-size-fits-all platitudes. The speaker was doing a great job of meeting both of those criteria at the same time. Marty noticed there were registration cards and pens in the seat backs in front of him. He pulled one of the cards out, grabbed the pen, and begin scribbling a quick note to Jane, who was evidently extremely interested in what was being said.

"Let's get out of here," Marty wrote. And placed the card discreetly in Jane's lap. Just then, rain began to fall, making its presence felt on the tin roof above them. Marty looked over to see if Jane had acknowledged that paper in her lap and saw that she now had her eyes closed, like she was tuning into a frequency nobody else heard.

He watched her for a moment before clicking the pen closed and poking her in the thigh with it. She casually opened her eyes and looked over at him, smiling. With his eyes, he directed her attention down to the note he had placed in her lap. She picked it up and held it just high enough to read what it said. Without looking at Marty, she held out her hand indicating she needed the pen to respond. Marty quickly placed it in her hand and awaited her response.

She wrote something down and gave the card back to Marty and then closed her eyes again.

"I want to stay for just a bit longer. I like listening to the rain hit the roof. It's sounds neat."

Sounds neat. Marty thought, curious about Jane's use of such a primitive adjective. He didn't know why, but he loved it. It was the cutest thing in the world. *It does sound neat.* Marty agreed.

After a few more minutes, Jane poked Marty on the leg and indicated she was ready to leave. The two excused themselves and walked out the back of the house. It was raining steadily outside. "Wait here and I'll bring the car around." Marty said. But, almost before he could finish his statement, Jane took off running to the car in the rain.

"Hey, wait up!" Marty shouted and then took off after her. He caught her just as they reached her truck. He unlocked the door for her and she climbed up on the passenger side. He jogged around to the driver's side and joined her in the car.

"What would you like to do now?" Marty said, starting to put the keys in the ignition.

Jane reached forward and placed her hand on Marty's, stopping him from cranking the car. "Let's just sit here for a while, listening to the rain." She said, as she scooted over to the middle and placed her head on Marty's chest. He put his arm around her and closed his eyes. He thought about how fortunate he was to be there with her, to smell her hair, the feel her face against his body, to know she wanted to be with him more than anything in the world.

"You know, you have what the speaker was talking about." Marty said after a few minutes of silence.

"What do you mean?"

"Inner strength. I've never known anyone as strong as you are. It's kind of annoying, actually." Marty teased.

"And why is that, mister?" Jane said, pretending to be offended.

"Because I'm supposed to be the strong one, your hero, the knight in shining armor. But you're *my* hero. Every time you come around, I feel weak inside. My heart goes haywire and my knees wobble. Nobody has ever made me feel so strong and so helpless at the same time. It's a mystery, really."

Jane sat up and looked into Marty's eyes, tears forming at the edge of hers. She leaned in and kissed him deeply before pulling back and placing her head back on his chest.

"Well let's be a mystery, then." Jane said.

"I'll be your weakness, and you'll be my strength."

~~~ ~~~ ~~~ ~~~ ~~~ ~~~ ~~~

Pulling back up to the park, Marty chained his bike at one of the designated bike areas and walked to the closest bench. He sat down and opened the puzzle book to the first crossword. This is when it dawned on him that he had no pen. *Wow. All this effort and I can't even write any answers down.* Marty put the book down beside him for a few minutes. He closed his eyes and felt the sun and slight breeze on his face. He listened to the sounds of people jogging, talking, playing. He watched some of them. They all looked so happy. Multitudes of people with memories fully intact. He wondered if they knew how fortunate they were.

How could they know? People take all manner of luxuries for granted. So many mysterious and complex and wonderful things utilized without a second thought given to how important, how essential they are to the joy and meaning of existence. He had never once considered how vital memory is to life experience.

Until he was in danger of losing it forever.

Marty picked up the crossword book and flipped to a random page in the middle. He started solving the puzzle in his head.

1-Across. 7 letters. INNER STRENGTH.

Stamina. Marty answered after pondering it for a minute.

6-Across. 7 letters. ENIGMA.

Mystery.

13-Across. 5 letters. INFORMATION STORAGE DEVICE.

CD ROM.

Marty set the book down as a new possibility came to him suddenly. Something he couldn't believe he hadn't thought of before. His heart rate increased, his body temperature rose, and adrenaline flooded his bloodstream. He was thinking back to he and Ben's visit to the Professor's abandoned house. There was a CD left behind for them to find. It had never occurred to him to pop it into a computer to see if there was anything else on it.

What if...what if there was more information on that disc than just a song?

Marty had kept the music CD they found in the Professor's house - even though Ben didn't see any need for it - for two reasons. One, the song on the CD was the most beautiful song he had ever heard, and something happened inside him when he heard it, although he wasn't quite sure what. And two, because he believed there had to be a reason the Professor had left it behind, on repeat. It was the only thing that made sense. He brought it home with him and kept it in the drawer of the old night stand by his bed.

I've got to get home and find out.

Marty folded the crossword puzzle book and placed it back in his rear pocket, mounted his bike, and began pedaling toward his house. His mind was racing, thinking about all of the possibilities, while at the same time trying to temper his expectations in case there wasn't anything there at all. But if there was…

There had to be! *Calm down, Marty. There are no guarantees.*

He parked his bike without bothering to lock it and sprinted up the three flights of stairs to his apartment. He pulled the keys from his right front pocket and as he went to put the key in the lock he dropped them on the ground. He swore and bent down to pick them up. He tried again and opened the door so hard it hit the wall and bounced back a little, staying wide open as Marty rushed into his bedroom.

He went straight for the nightstand, his heart racing from the rush of the physical activity and the anticipation of what he might find. He pulled the disc out and went to the other room to get his laptop. He sat down on the couch, resting the computer on his legs and popped the CD into the player on the side of the computer. *Come on, come on.* Marty thought, impatient for the CD player to warm up. It was only a few seconds before a dialogue box appeared on the screen asking what Marty would like to do with the CD. Marty clicked "Open Folder to View Files" and held his breath as he heard the machine start spinning the disc faster. It was searching for whatever might or might not be there.

Just moments later, another window opened to reveal two files. One was a music file titled "Con te Partiro." The other was a .jpeg file labeled with the number five. Marty's heart jumped when his eyes rested on the second file.

There was something else on there!

"Please, please, please be something helpful, " Marty said out loud as he double clicked on the file. Immediately the picture popped up on the screen and Marty couldn't believe what he was looking at.

It was a map with a red dot.

Chapter Sixteen

"Nothing that you have not given away will ever be really yours." - C.S. Lewis

When Marty arrived at the dot on the map, an abandoned construction site on the outskirts of town, there was only one structure. It was a mobile building that at one time must have been the base of operations for the project's contractor. He rolled his bike to the building and leaned it up against the side. He noticed the number five hanging crooked on the right of the trailer. *This must be the place.* Walking to the door, he looked around to make sure nobody else was there. He climbed the wooden steps that creaked loudly beneath him, startling him and causing him to go slower and put less pressure on his feet on his way up to the door.

He knocked.

No answer.

He knocked several times more and still nothing. *Don't know why I expected anything different. There's never anyone there. Somebody is playing some messed up game with me.*

He tried the door knob and it was locked. *No more open doors. Guess I have to open them myself now.*

Marty retreated down the steps and looked around for some sort of tool or implement with which to break into the office. There was no dead bolt, just a knob. After looking around for a few minutes and finding nothing satisfactory, he went over to a pile of cinder blocks and picked one up with both hands. He carried it up the steps outside the trailer door, this time not worried about the noise he was making.

When he reached the door, he lifted the cinder block up and brought its weight down on the door handle as hard as he could. The sound of the impact echoed loudly through the abandoned work site. Marty looked around instinctively before checking to see if the force of the blow did any damage. It had. The door knob had jarred loose from its setting. One or two more hits and it should come free.

It only took one more hit with the cinder block and the cheaply-made door knob fell to the ground at Marty's feet. Marty pushed the door open slowly and took a quick look around inside. From where he stood, the only thing he could see in the entire trailer was an air-conditioning unit in the back window, *it's hard to believe nobody has stolen that thing,* and a no-frills desk - probably purchased from one of those do-it-yourself furniture superstores - with a rolling chair behind it. Marty entered the trailer to get a more complete look of the place.

Nothing else.

The fan from the A/C unit clicked on suddenly, causing Marty to jump. *How is there still power running to this place? And why?* He walked over to the window and switched the unit to the "off" position and then meandered over to the desk, opening the two drawers on the left side. Empty. *Of course. Another dead end.*

Marty slouched down into the chair behind the desk, and pulled his memory journal from the back of his jeans. He opened it and went to the bottom of the list. Another memory gone. He scratched it off with the pen he now stashed inside the journal, then raised up to put the book back in its place. When he came back to a sitting position, he felt his foot brush up against something below him. He looked down and noticed a section of folded up newspaper resting next to his shoe. He picked it up and looked at it. It was *The Herald*, the city's flagship daily. Marty bought it every day, mostly for the crossword puzzles, but it didn't seem normal to him. The text was different, the color of the paper seemed odd, it was formatted differently. His eyes moved to the corner of the page, looking for the date.

The paper was ten years old. *A lot of good that's going to do me,* Marty thought and dropped the paper back on the floor. He sat at the desk, wondering what Ben had been up to these last few days. He pulled his phone out to check it. No messages, no missed calls, no e-mails. *Hate it when that happens.*

Marty reached down and picked up the paper once again. He began to thumb through it, unable to concentrate on any one picture or article. Until he got to the second-to-last page. The headline of the column in the bottom left corner was manually highlighted in yellow.

MAN SENDS WIFE SAME BIRTHDAY CARD FOR FIFTY YEARS

~~~ ~~~ ~~~ ~~~ ~~~ ~~~ ~~~

"How did you get this *again*?" Jane was sincerely mystified.

"I have my ways." Marty said.

"I hid it in a place I just knew you would never think to look. I didn't tell anyone else where I hid it except…"

The light went on inside Jane's head. "No way. I can't believe my sister told you where I hid it!"

"Now wait a minute. Don't go jumping to conclusions. I never said anything about Joy. I just said 'I have my ways.'"

"Yeah, you have *ways* all right. *A* way. My back-stabbing little sister!"

"I'm not conceding anything. I think you'll just have to get used to the fact that I will always find it. Besides, I think you wanted me to find it. It's kind of my unique thing. It's thoughtful. It's...*charming.*"

"Charming? Charming that you're too cheap to buy me a new card anytime a special occasion comes around? *Charming*, indeed." Jane said, with a heavy dose of playfulness.

But Marty was right and they both knew it. Hiding the card had become her part in this little game he had started with her. It began on the first birthday she had after they began dating. Marty had dropped by her apartment early in the morning and placed an envelope on her windshield. Jane came down to get in her car to go to class and found the slightly oversized card waiting for her. On the inside, it said,

"Don't worry about the past, because you can't change it. Don't worry about the future, because it will be bright. Don't worry about the present, because I didn't get you one." Marty had signed it, "My future is bright because it includes you. Happy Birthday, Janie. Love, Me."

Of course, he had presents for her when they met for dinner later that evening. But he needed a general, somewhat funny, and very cheesy greeting to be printed on the inside. This wouldn't be just an ordinary card.

When Marty was younger, he had read a newspaper article about a man who had been sending his wife the same birthday card for fifty years. Every birthday, he would locate the card, scribble a new note on it, and put it in the mail. Marty thought it was brilliant and decided right then if he ever got married, he would do the exact same thing.

And even though he and Jane weren't married, they would be eventually if Marty had any say in it. So he decided he would start the process, only he would take it a step further. He was going to send the same card for any special occasion. Birthdays, Valentine's Day, Anniversaries, Christmas, and even Mother's Day eventually. In the beginning, he had to rely on her level of sentimentality. If she was the type to save cards, he would be in luck. If not, then the whole idea was doomed from the start.

Fortunately for Marty, Jane kept the card. She even tacked it to the bulletin board in her room, making the first steal relatively easy. He didn't have to locate it because he knew exactly where it was. When she came down on Valentine's Day and found the same card on her windshield with a new note from Marty, she was equal parts amused and confused. *What is he doing?* She thought with a smile on her face.

"You gave me the same card, nerd." Jane said to him later that day.

"I know," he responded with a mischievous grin. "But it had a new note in it."

"Yes, it was very sweet. Thank you."

"You're welcome, Love."

When the one-year anniversary of their dating rolled around, Jane had forgotten about the card, which she had placed in a scrapbook the day after Valentine's Day. When she walked down to her car that morning, she just shook her head and laughed. He'd done it again.

Ever since then, she had started hiding the card, in more and more elaborate and difficult-to-locate places. If Marty was going to continue with this tradition, he was going to have to work for it. She would make him work for it. How bad did he want it? She would find out. Christmas, Birthday, Valentine's Day, Anniversary, for the better part of three years, every time the card would somehow show up on her windshield.

On the morning of her twenty-second birthday, she came down to her car, confident the card would not be there. She had defeated him. Victory was hers. And she would be able to gloat, but only for a little while. Then she would give him the card, let him add a note, and then hide it again for the next occasion. That was the plan, anyway.

Until she approached her car and saw the familiar envelope sitting there where it always did. *How in the world? He did it again.*

Jane immediately picked up the phone and called Marty, shaking her head and chuckling to herself as the phone rang.

~~~ ~~~ ~~~ ~~~ ~~~ ~~~ ~~~

Marty was shaking his head as he finished reading about the man who had sent his wife the same birthday card every year for the past fifty years. He wondered if the man (and his wife) were still alive, him still sending the card, her still receiving it. He hoped so. *I like this guy's style. I just might have to do the same one day. Thanks for the idea, sir.*

Marty enjoyed a rare laugh as he picked up the phone to try to get in touch with Ben. As it was ringing, he flipped to the back page of the paper and saw a ten-year old ad for a bookstore having a huge sale. *This was back when people actually read paper books. How did we live that way?* Marty joked to himself. He continued reading, "All books, including new releases, up to thirty percent off.*" *An asterisk, always an asterisk.*

There, in the middle of the quarter-page advertisement, was an address for the bookstore.

And the address was marked by the same yellow highlighter.

Chapter Seventeen

"Time moves in one direction, memory in another." - William Gibson

It took Marty a few tries to get Ben to answer his phone. When they finally connected, Ben began to try and explain why he had been so hard to get in touch with, but Marty wouldn't let him get started before he interrupted with the news of an address. He told him of the crossword puzzle and the map image hidden on the CD and about the 10-year old newspaper under the desk of the abandoned office trailer. His sentences were spilling out so fast he was running out of breath at the end of each one.

When he got to the part about the highlighted address, Ben simply said, "Text me the address you are at. I'll pick you up in thirty minutes." And he hung up the phone. *That was abrupt.* Marty sent the information to Ben and waited on the steps of the office trailer, grateful he had picked up the trail again, but becoming more and more anxious about his fading memories. He pulled the journal out and scanned the list. There weren't many bullet points remaining. It was like watching the clock on a bomb ticking down under a minute. He fought hard to push back the panic and fear creeping along the edges of his soul.

Ben pulled up twenty seven minutes after he hung up the phone with Marty. He pulled the car around so the passenger door was on Marty's side. The window was already rolled down. "You look like hell." Ben called out, only half-joking. "Thanks. You look like a homeless lumberjack." Marty responded, rising to his feet and walking toward the door. He opened it and slid into the passenger seat. He'd been in this seat on many goose chases in the past couple of weeks. He was hoping this wasn't more of the same.

"Did you miss me?" Ben joked.

"No, but I missed the feeling of failure accompanying all of our adventures."

"Close enough. Let's get this latest spectacular flop over with. Let me see the paper."

Marty showed Ben the highlighted address. "Interesting," was Ben's insightful response.

"That was deep. Alright, give me a second to figure out where this puppy is located."

Marty placed the paper in his lap, studied it, and started mapping out a route. The sound of the idling engine continued to click as Ben sat patiently in the driver's seat. "Which way?" Ben asked, finally breaking the silence. Marty was in the passenger seat with a map of the city in his lap. He was staring down at the paper, but his mind was elsewhere. "Huh?" was his disconnected response.

"Say which way," Ben tried again. Marty's head popped up from the page and quickly looked over him. "Wait. Repeat what you just said."

"Say which way!"

~~~ ~~~ ~~~ ~~~ ~~~ ~~~ ~~~

Jane pulled up in her older model Ford Bronco. In its prime, it had been a nice white, but after twenty-plus years of use it was slightly darker, more of a cream color. Marty loved this car, but what he loved even more was her in this car. There was something about a woman who chose to drive an old truck like this. He smiled at her as she swung around to position him on the passenger side and reached over to unlock the door. He hopped in and leaned over to kiss her on the cheek.

"Hey babe!" she started.

"Hey yourself! What do you want to do today?" he asked.

"I dunno. I've got to be at work in five hours, so whatever we do, we need to keep in mind I need to be back in town by five."

"That does eliminate some things. I suppose we have to stay within state lines. No flights or train rides. No trips to the shore. Hmmmm." And he did his best to think up an adventure for the afternoon. She just sat in the driver's seat looking at him, waiting for him to come up with a plan. He knew she was watching him, and he tried to exaggerate his thinking-up-a-plan face so she would believe he was trying really hard. Or she would laugh. Or both.

"Did you remember I only have five hours?" she teased and giggled, as he continued to sit there thinking. He tried to convince himself that if he'd had a few hours to come up with something, he could have thought of a great adventure. But the truth was, he wasn't a planner. He liked to move freely without a schedule, so this should have been in his wheelhouse. But the pressure of the moment, and her beautiful, demanding eyes, made it nearly impossible for him to think of anything good.

She could tell he wasn't making any progress, so she made a suggestion. "How about this," she began, "I'll start driving and every time we come to an intersection, you tell me which way to go. Forward, left, or right, depending on the options. Then we'll just see where this day takes us." He turned slowly toward her, moving his eyes faster than his head and a satisfied and relieved smile began to emerge on his face. *This woman is magical*, he thought. But he didn't say it out loud. "Sounds like a plan, Ms. Carson. Let's get this adventure started!"

"Okay!" she said in a silly voice. She put the car in drive and began to edge the Bronco in the direction of the parking lot exit. When they reached it, she pressed her foot to the brake and looked over at him. It was time to make the first turn. "Right" he said rather quickly, without thinking about it. She put her blinker on and the car moved out onto the street heading south toward the highway. When they came to the first stop light, he called out "left" and they went left.

It went on like this for a while. Right, left, straight, left, straight, straight, right, left, straight. Sometimes, on longer stretches of road, they would get lost in conversation or some silly story so when they reached an intersection he briefly forgot the game. She would sit there for a few seconds until he remembered and called out the next direction. She would laugh a bit and then follow his command. It was an hour or so before they hit the stretch of road Marty had decided to take her to.

It was a state road winding along a river, as if the two were a couple of ropes laid out side by side and tied

together with string at certain points. The strings were the bridges crossing the water. Every time they passed a bridge, they would stop. He would pull her expensive camera off the floorboard of the back seat and take photographs of her standing on the bridges, water flowing below, trickling or rushing, falling toward the secret places only rivers go.

The sky was brilliant and blue, with clouds perfectly drawn. *Looks like a cartoon film sky,* he thought to himself as he continued to snap photos of Jane on their fourth bridge stop. This thought pleased him and caused a song from the movie to pop into his head. He began singing it out loud, dramatically, for effect, like the singer on the soundtrack. He crooned away dramatically, making her already big smile turn into laughter.

The camera kept time with the singing. Click, click, click.

~~~ ~~~ ~~~ ~~~ ~~~ ~~~ ~~~

Click, click, click, went the car's engine as Marty finally figured out the route they should take.

"Ok. Looks like we are going to take a left when we get back up to the main road."

"Then what?"

"I'll tell you when we get there. No need to give you the next direction until you need it."

Chapter Eighteen

"Betrayal is the only truth that sticks." - Arthur Miller

When Ben pulled the car into the parking lot, their anticipation of what they might find was being mitigated by two factors.

One was the condition of the strip mall they were looking at. It was abandoned, and had been for many years. Every store, presumably once a thriving business, was empty. Paint faded and peeling, "For Rent" or "Closed" signs in the windows, signs with crooked or missing letters. Tufts of grass were growing up through cracks in the pavement. Not a car in sight. They were just on the other side of town, but this part of the city hadn't done well. It had a look and feel closer to a third world country. It didn't seem likely they would find anyone here. Perhaps it had all been a coincidence. The highlighted portions of the paper were just random notes of a reader ten years ago who left the paper on the ground, never thinking it would be found.

This pessimism they both felt was a direct result of the second factor. Namely that they had been disappointed on several occasions already, Ben even more so than Marty. There was no reason to believe this lead would be any different than all of the others. They had made a nasty habit of chasing rabbits and sniffing out the most excruciating of dead ends. It was almost an art form, it seemed. They were the anti-detectives, able to take any solid lead and turn it into a black hole.

Ben and Marty scanned the old strip mall for the number on the paper, but numbers were hard to find. Most of the buildings had been dormant for years. Paint or stickers used to indicate street numbers had mostly vanished. They decided their best bet was to get out and walk the front of the strip mall, checking each door, looking in every window until they either found what they were looking for or walked away empty-handed again.

But when Ben pulled closer to the end of the long building, Marty noticed a door that had a still, if just barely, visible number on the top.

2100.

He flinched and poked his head out the window to make sure he wasn't mistaken. He wasn't. "There it is." Marty said, almost not believing what his eyes saw.

Ben said nothing, but the look on his face made Marty suddenly uneasy again. He brushed it off and focused on the possibilities of what could be just on the other side of that door.

Ben parked the car right where they were. Marty got out and waited on the curb for Ben to come around, and they both just stood there for a minute or two, unsure of how to proceed. Marty assumed Ben would take the lead, but it seemed he was waiting on Marty to go in first. Ben was standing just behind Marty at his left shoulder, more like a bodyguard than an equal.

Marty looked back at Ben, took a deep breath, and began moving towards the glass door. When he got right in front of it, he paused. They could not see in because the frosted glass obscured their view. Marty reached to pull on the metal handle, fully expecting it to be locked. Every other door he had come to had required either muscle or miracle to open. He gave it a tug and was shocked to feel the door open easily.

He gave Ben an *are you kidding me?* look and walked slowly through the door, holding it for Ben who was right behind him. Inside the large open room was what looked like a laboratory. Towards the back of the room, there was a predictable sight - another dentist chair with a light over the top. Nearby, at a table filled with various medical supplies, a familiar figure turned from what he was doing to face the two men.

Marty and Ben stood next to each other, the reality of the Professor right in front of them taking its time to register. He was in a lab coat, with a white shirt and blue tie, and neatly pressed khaki business slacks. As astonished as they both were to see him, he was not at all surprised to see them, at least he wasn't giving any visible cues to suggest so.

The sight of the Professor caused Marty's hope to stir. *I've got a chance. It may be just a sliver of hope, but it's not over yet. I still have one memory left. The Professor is right here. He can help me get my memory back. He can tell me what to do. He has to.*

Marty spoke first.

"We've been looking everywhere for you. I've lost every memory of my life except one. I need your help. We need your help." Marty motioned to Ben, for some reason. As if the Professor would be more apt to help if both of

217

them were desperate. The truth was, it was too late for Ben. And, somehow, he sensed the Professor would know that anyway.

"I don't need your help."

It was Ben. His voice suddenly cold, vengeful.

To Marty's horror, he pulled out a gun that had been tucked into the back waist band of his jeans and raised it, pointing it right at the Professor.

"Ben, what are you doing?" Marty shouted, deep fear washing over him.

"What I came here for."

"This isn't what we came here for. If you hurt him, I have no chance. You said you wanted to help me."

Ben turned to Marty, his face different, uncovered, full of vengeance.

"I know what I said. I said what I needed to for you to help me find this monster. And now, I've found him. He took everything from me. EVERYTHING!" He suddenly screamed. "And now, I'm going to take everything from him."

"Ben, you can't do this!" Marty pleaded, as all of the suspicions and gut feelings he'd had about Ben ever since they met came flooding back to him in vivid detail. He *can* do this. *This* is what he has been after since the beginning.

Marty felt used. And stupid. But what else could he have done? Ben had done what Marty needed him to do as well. He was standing just a few feet away from potential deliverance.

Only he didn't have a gun.

"I have what you need." the Professor finally spoke.

He was looking directly at Marty.

"What is it you have? What do I need?" Marty asked, anxious, feeling as hopeless and desperate as ever.

"I have the box containing all of your memories," the Professor said with a remarkably calm demeanor., as if it were a banana pointed at him by a harmless monkey and not a gun by a man bent on revenge.

"He's lying. That's all he does is LIE. You said yourself: you watched it burn." Ben countered, directing his words at Marty, but never taking his eyes, or the gun, off the Professor.

Marty *had* said that. And he thought for sure he had watched it burn in the twilight between full consciousness and sleep he had encountered just before the Professor did, whatever it was he did to put Marty under. But he could have been mistaken.

"Maybe I made a mistake. It's worth a shot. Please, Ben." Marty was begging.

It was a useless attempt.

"He's just trying to save his own skin," Ben said. "He burned your memories just like he did mine. You think he would save the evidence? We could sue him. Even press criminal charges. Those boxes are nothing but ash in a fireplace. And I will never let him burn me again."

"Ben, no!" Marty shouted in desperation. But it was too late. Ben's eyes were full of rage and he wasn't going to let anyone or anything stand in his way.

He walked calmly over to Marty, and said, "I'm sorry, Marty. But I can't have you ruining this for me." As the last word came out of his mouth, Marty could see Ben raising the gun over his head and the butt of the weapon coming down hard on the top of Marty's head. The force of the blow was staggering, and he wobbled for a few seconds before crumpling near Ben's feet.

The blow rendered Marty on the precipice of unconsciousness as he helplessly watched Ben and the Professor charge at each other. Through blurred vision, he saw a struggle ensue between the two men that seemed to go on for a long time, as if in slow motion, with Ben struggling to get his gun in position to fire, and the Professor holding the gun away from him, attempting to dislodge it from Ben's hand.

A shot rang out, echoing through the entire room. It was so loud. Deafeningly loud.

Marty hung on long enough to see one body fall to the ground.

No.

As he lost consciousness, he couldn't decide which one of them he wished were still standing.

Chapter Nineteen

"Who looks outside, dreams; who looks inside, awakes." - Carl Jung

~~~ ~~~ ~~~ ~~~ ~~~ ~~~ ~~~

Marty stood on the balcony of his apartment, his eyes focused on the figure three stories below. A person, laying face down, their blood staining the grass. The image of the person was hazy, but he could tell it was a man. Horrified, he sprinted out of his apartment and rushed down the stairs to figure out what happened. Outside, emergency personnel and police were milling about, gathering evidence from the scene, wrapping up their duties. Nobody was paying any attention to Marty.

It was as if he wasn't even there.

He walked closer and closer to the scene, expecting someone to stop him, but no one did. When he got within a few feet, a few police officers walked past him and gathered around the body. Together they began to lift it up, as if they were doing it just for Marty, until he could see the disfigured face of someone he knew very well.

Oh no.

~~~ ~~~ ~~~ ~~~ ~~~ ~~~ ~~~

Marty awoke from his dream with a sharp headache and reached up to feel the tender knot on his head where Ben had struck him with the butt of the gun. He was back in the living room of his apartment. And he had no idea how he had gotten there.

The throbbing nodule on his skull was a clear reminder of what transpired before he passed out. He was attacked by Ben, someone he had come to foolishly trust, who had gone after the Professor with intent to harm, perhaps to end his life. One of them had suffered a gunshot wound, he was pretty sure he remembered a loud noise and seeing one of the two men fall. As much as he had come to care for Ben as a person, Marty hoped with all of his heart it was the Professor who was still standing. If Ben was shot, it was his own fault. He had let vengeance and rage take root in his heart. Those seeds never grow into anything good.

Should he try Ben's number? What if Ben was successful in gunning down the Professor and was on the run? Would he even answer? If he did, would he give Marty any information? Or would he lie? And how would Marty know the difference? It didn't seem like a phone call to Ben would do much good, but Marty concluded there wasn't a better starting place than to at least attempt to connect with Ben. He reached down and felt around in his pockets to find his cell phone. It wasn't on him. He felt around the couch he was on when he woke up. It wasn't there, either. *Great, I've lost my phone. Now what?*

He stood up from the couch, his knees were wobbly and the movement caused his aching head to pound even harder. *I need something for this headache.* Marty shuffled into the kitchen and retrieved the bottle of painkiller from the cabinet by the refrigerator, and shook out four pills into his hand. He put them into his mouth while he grabbed a glass from another cabinet, filled it halfway with tap water, and drank it down along with the medicine. *Without a phone, my only play is to get back to the Professor's warehouse location.*

Walking into the other bedroom, Marty sat down at the desk and did a search for a local cab company to pick him up. He didn't remember the exact address, but he could definitely tell the driver how to get there. He estimated it would be about a $35-40 cab fare. He reached in his pocket to see if he had any money. To his relief, his wallet and driver's license were in his pocket. Unfortunately, he only had five one dollar bills. Not enough.

He usually kept a couple of hundred dollars in a wooden cigar box that served as a bookend on the shelf above the computer. Marty stood up, leaning over the desk, and pulled the box from its spot. In doing so, the closest book to the box fell over and made a slapping sound as it hit the wood of the shelf. It was a book Marty was familiar with, a green shiny cover he knew very well.

Distracted from his original purpose, Marty took the book down from the shelf and sat back down in the chair, placing the box absent-mindedly on the desk. In his hands was a copy of Shel Silverstein's *The Giving Tree. H*is father used to read to him at night when he was growing up. Although he didn't remember its significance anymore, he was curious about it, since it was the only children's book among the five or six books sitting above the desk in the spare bedroom that served as an "office" in his two-bedroom apartment.

He opened it up and began to read.

Once there was a tree…
And she loved a little boy

And on he read…

But the boy stayed away for a long time.
And when he came back,
the tree was so happy
she could hardly speak.

When Marty turned the next page, a picture resting inside the book came loose and fell down into his lap.

It was the picture of a young woman. Brown hair, her head back, laughing at the camera, brown eyes ablaze with joy. She was standing on a bridge, and the sun was slowly setting behind her. She was absolutely stunning.

On the back of the picture was a simple sentence. And even though it had no context for Marty at the moment, it took his breath away.

"Across bridges, over rivers, and on into the setting sun, I will ride anywhere with you." - M.J.

Marty found himself crying, having no idea why. *This must be her. Why would I ever want to forget her?*

He put the picture in his front shirt pocket, opened the cigar box, retrieved several $20 bills, and hopped out of the chair.

I've got to get back to the Professor.

Chapter Twenty

"Little things console us because little things afflict us." - Blaise Pascal

Marty handed cash to the cab driver and climbed out of the passenger side of the taxi he had taken back to the Professor's location. The bright morning sun greeted him as he emerged from the back seat, causing him to reach instinctively for sunglasses that weren't hanging between the buttons of his shirt. His head was still pounding. But he was as determined as ever, and nothing was going to stop him now.

Marty found the front door to the building propped open with a rubber stopper. He entered into the main room and found the Professor in his lab coat, standing near the dentist's chair. It seemed as if he was waiting for Marty to arrive, like he knew Marty was coming right then. There was no need to dance around the obvious, so Marty didn't even say hello before getting to the point of his return.

"You said you have what I need. And I think what I need more than anything is to remember the woman in this picture." Marty said, taking the picture from his shirt pocket and holding it up for the Professor to see.

The Professor nodded and then motioned for Marty to sit down in the dentist's chair.

Marty hesitated for a moment, before deciding he had nothing to lose. If this man could take away his memory, then there was no reason to believe he couldn't bring it back. "So how's this going to work?" he asked.

"Well, it's quite simple, really. I didn't actually get rid of your memories. I just re-wired the connections a little bit so your conscious mind wouldn't be able to recall them. I hid them, so to speak, in your subconscious. You may have had dreams about her, because when we're asleep our brains ignore the rules they follow when we're awake."

"I did dream about her. On at least two occasions I can remember. Or at least I think I did."

"And you woke up feeling like you had spent time with someone you knew well, someone you loved very much?"

"Yes."

"Good. What I'm going to do now is reverse the procedure. I'll reconnect the right synapses and put the memories back where they're supposed to be. Your neurons will begin to fire in the patterns they are familiar with, connections will be resumed, and your entire memory will be restored."

"All of it?"

"Yes, all of it."

"Ok, I don't want to waste another second. Let's get this done."

The Professor began to rub Marty's head on either side near the temples, just as he had done the first time. It was only a matter of moments before Marty found himself getting very sleepy. He was staring at the picture he found inside the book, which he was holding in between his hands resting on his chest. As he drifted into unconsciousness, the picture slipped out of his hands. The Professor caught it before it hit the ground and placed it in the pocket of his lab coat.

When Marty woke up this time, he wasn't alone on a bus stop bench. He was still reclining in the chair. Through blurry eyes, he could see the Professor walking over to check on him. The closer he got, the more he came into focus. Marty was emerging from his stupor quite well, and he felt as if he were a new person. Somehow his head seemed clearer, more focused, renewed.

"How are you feeling?" the Professor asked.

"Pretty damn good, actually. Better than the first time for sure. When I woke up on that bus bench I was disoriented and I had a pounding headache. I guess I expected something similar this time."

"Before, you were veering away from the brain's natural, intended course. Now you've put it back where it was supposed to be. Those memories, no matter how painful they may be, are a part of who you are. They are there to shape you, to make you into the person you are supposed to be. They can infuse you with compassion and humility and, hopefully, gratitude. These are the characteristics that renew our minds and strengthen our hearts."

"It's hard to understand those things when all you feel is despair and hopelessness."

"Yes. But the most beautiful and lasting things in life emerge from the darkness of despair and hopelessness. These experiences are how we understand each other, how we feel each other, how we help each other survive and grow. It is the way of things."

The Professor pulled the picture of Jane out of his pocket and handed it to Marty. Marty looked at it and smiled through the tears beginning to form at the corner of his eyes. He pressed it against his heart and laid there for a few moments.

Jane.

After several minutes passed, Marty swung his legs around so he was sitting up on the side of the chair and wiped the corners of his eyes with the backs of his wrists.

"There was a box. Where is the box? The box I gave you before I went through the first procedure? You said you still have it. Do you?" Marty asked, a deep need rising up in him.

The Professor nodded and motioned to a box sitting on the floor in the corner of the room. Marty rushed over to it and slid on his knees, skidding right up next to it. He tore through the duct tape surrounding the top of the box and removed the lid as quickly as he could. He set it at an angle leaning against the wall, and placed the picture so that it was resting upright inside the box top, looking back at him.

One by one he removed the items from the file box, the box with JANE written on the outside in his own handwriting. He pulled out an oversized greeting card and read it, laughing through his tears. He found a used lottery ticket, an empty coffee cup, a CD with his name on it and the words "Con te Partiro" underneath it, both in Jane's handwriting. He found the note about the sound of the rain, a couple of poems she wrote, pictures she drew for him, birthday cards, a stuffed bunny rabbit with carrot pads for its paws, and more.

The last thing he removed was the laminated crossword puzzle, the thing that had started it all.

Chapter Twenty-One

"If you can only remember me with tears, then
don't remember me at all." - Laura Ingalls Wilder

Marty Drake remembered Jane Carson.

He remembered the day she ran into him at the coffee shop and the crossword puzzle bet. He remembered the first date. He remembered her singing the song, sounding just like an angel. He remembered how shocked he was when she had stolen coffee in the square, and how exhilarating it was to steal a cup himself, how she *always* left him feeling exhilarated. He remembered their first kiss in the canoe, carrying her after her hiking injury, and the trip taking pictures by bridges. He remembered the lottery game and the card he sent her every special occasion. He remembered shopping for his sister's wedding gift and how Jane loved the sound of the rain on a tin roof. He remembered the cadence of her laugh and the curl of her lips when she pretended to pout, and the sheer brilliance of her brown eyes.

God, those brown eyes.

He remembered how she called him "babe," the smell and taste of her skin, how she ran her fingers through his hair when they were sitting close.

Marianna Jane Carson, MJ, Janie, Carson, Sweet Love, Baby.

He remembered her.

And he remembered why he had to forget her in the first place.

The pain came washing back anew, like a person who experiences something terrible and eventually cries themselves to sleep, only to wake up and have it flood horribly back all over again. He bent over from the shock of it all coming back to him. Nausea overtaking his stomach and sorrow engulfing his entire being.

Jane.

She was gone.

And he was to blame.

Or was he? He certainly had accepted the blame he had placed upon himself. Nobody else had been willing to do so. Her mom and siblings didn't blame him, his own family said there was no way he could have known, and the authorities certainly assigned no guilt to him. But none of that mattered. He had convicted himself. It was devastating enough to lose Jane, but to believe he was responsible for her death made it unbearable. Each and every day became a constant doling out of punishment upon himself.

"Would you like to talk about why you're sad?" It was the Professor's calm, soothing, sincere voice interrupting Marty's renewed anguish. There was a gentle and compassionate tone to his voice, why had Marty not noticed it the first time?

"I don't really want to, but I think maybe I should."

"I'm listening."

After a few minutes of silence, Marty gathered himself and began.

"Jane was everything to me. I had never met anyone who made me feel alive. It felt like we were made for each other. I knew we would spend the rest of our lives by each other's side. We would marry, travel the world, have a big family, grow old together. All I wanted was to make her feel loved, to make her feel beautiful, to make her happy. I never would have done anything, *anything* to intentionally bring her harm.

"And yet that's exactly what I did. The person who was supposed to protect her, to be the gatekeeper for her, ended up being the person who left the gate wide open." Small traces of tears began to crawl down Marty's cheeks. It was back - the pain he sought to erase, to bury, had risen again. His heart spasmed within his chest as he spoke.

The Professor handed Marty a tissue and probed, "Go on."

Marty took the cloth and dabbed his cheeks as he continued.

"Ever since I was a kid, I had this overwhelming feeling of compassion for people who couldn't walk normally. When I would see people struggling to walk, something myself and everyone else just takes for granted, it would, I don't know, it would *do something* inside me. So many times I felt compelled to show compassion to a person I would see in that condition. You can usually kind of tell who is just going through a difficult stretch or a temporary injury and will be back to walking normally eventually. Those weren't the people who made my insides cry out to help them. For years, I just lived with this internal battle. It wouldn't present itself very often anyway. Most people have no trouble walking.

"Then one day a guy showed up at the grocery store I frequented as a student. He was a greeter, gathered carts, did all of the things grunts on the bottom of the rung do. He had a kind face, his speech was slurred, and the way he walked when he went to get the carts looked so awkward and painful. But he always had a smile on his face and he seemed to go about his job as if he loved it, as though it was the most important job in the world. Every time I would go to the grocery store, he was there, smiling, offering kind words in his slow speech, doing his job, this menial job, with such joy and kindness. And every time I saw him walk, my gut just wrenched. I wished for him to be able to walk normally.

"Eventually, those gestures weren't enough. I wanted to know this guy. To befriend him. To let him know he wasn't broken, that his spirit challenged me and encouraged me every time I saw him. So I started going up to the grocery store even when I didn't have anything to buy. I'd make up excuses to go there and engage him in conversation. His name was Ronny. I found out he liked coffee, so I started bringing him coffee. Then I started coordinating with his break. I would bring the coffee and we would talk about his life. I finally told him what an inspiration he had been to me, even before I knew his name or who he was. And that I wanted to help him, if he needed help. I didn't want to assume he couldn't function completely on his own. I had more than enough evidence he could. But we all need friendship, we all need to feel valued, we all need a feeling of home.

"Over time, we became good friends. Even I was surprised at the kind of things I was sharing about my past and my struggles with a person whose level of understanding was much lower than any of the friends I'd ever had. And he would share with me, how difficult it was to live life with legs that didn't work exactly how they were supposed to work, the constant ridicule and the meanness of people, the lack of understanding, the lack of belonging, the absence of home.

"The first time Ronny met Jane, she did not have a good feeling about him. She had some sort of intuition he wasn't good for me. She felt he looked at her in an inappropriate way, and she didn't want to be around him. 'He gives me the creeps,' she would say. At the time, I was disappointed with her. How could she be so insensitive, so unaware her bias was a result of his handicap? It made me question who she was, and in some moments, whether or not I could be with her.

"But I continued my friendship with Ronny, nonetheless. I hoped once she became comfortable around him, Jane's attitude towards him would change. Sometimes I would invite him along if Jane and I were going out for dinner or to an event I thought he might like. And, for the most part, she didn't say much about it. Occasionally, later she would say he had been staring at her, but lots of guys stared at Jane. She was remarkably beautiful. So I just kind of chalked it up to guys being guys."

"You listened, but didn't *hear* what she was saying." the Professor said.

"Yeah. You said it well. I didn't hear her. At all. It wasn't long into our friendship when Ronny got kicked out of the place he was living and was in need of a place to stay. Since I had an extra room in my apartment, I offered for him to move in with me for a season, so long as he paid some of the rent with the money he earned from his job. And so we became roommates. Jane was not at all in favor of the idea. In the beginning, she said she might not come over as much., which made me angry and I accused her of letting stereotypes of mentally-challenged people cloud her judgment. She responded by asking why I didn't trust her, why I couldn't just believe what she was saying, why I was putting someone I barely knew in a place of priority over her. And there was quite a bit of friction between us for the first few weeks. But we loved each other. We wanted to be together. And eventually our relationship recovered. It became stronger than ever before.

"I bought a ring and began planning a semi-elaborate scheme to surprise her with it on the third anniversary of the day we bumped into each other in the coffee shop. I had a couple of my friends in on the plot, with specific roles to fill to make the occasion one Jane would never forget. On the night before it was to happen, I let Ronny know what my plans were. One of the parts of the plan required Jane to be at my apartment by herself for about an hour. I told Ronny he needed to be out of the house in the afternoon. He said it was fine because he was going to be at work anyway, but there was something off about his tone, his body language, like I had just delivered devastating news. I shrugged it off at the time because he could be extremely moody. He went back into his room and I didn't see him for the rest of the night.

"The next day, my friends and I were out and about taking care of various details for the engagement. I had instructed Jane to be at my apartment at four and to let herself in with her key. This wasn't unusual. She had come to my house many times before I got home from work or class so we could just go as soon as I got home. She would leave little notes here and there. Things to surprise me." Then it hit Marty: "That must be when she put the picture of herself in *The Giving Tree*," he said to himself. The thought brought tears to his eyes, waves of tears were stored up and waiting to come out, and he was trying desperately to get through the story before he became unglued.

He paused for a moment, gathering himself, wiping the corners of his eyes with his hands: "I apologize."

"No apology necessary," the Professor said.

After a few moments, Marty took a deep breath and continued. "Where was I? Oh, yes. Jane was supposed to be at my apartment by four p.m., under the assumption I would be home from work around 4:30 so we could make our evening plans. She had no idea the evening was already planned. It was to be the most exciting and memorable night of her life. But I never got the chance to make it happen for her. When my friend David showed up at my apartment to whisk her away to the first location, he let himself in with my key. When he turned the corner into the living room, he saw Ronny standing up over the couch. He was weeping uncontrollably and saying, 'I'm so sorry. I just wanted you to love me. I'm so sorry. I just wanted you to love me.'"

"David dashed over to see Jane laying on the ground, unconscious. He shouted, 'What did you do!' pushing Ronny down and out of the way. David was a Boy Scout and had extensive hours of EMT training after high school. If anyone could save her, it would have been him. He tried frantically to revive her, before he paused a moment to dial 911. And he then went right back to work on Jane, fighting for her, desperately trying to bring her back. I'll never stop being grateful for that. Despite his efforts, she would never breathe again."

His words trailed off softly as he said them.

At this point, the tears were flowing steadily down Marty's shirt; much of it collecting at his collar, the rest continuing on down his chest and stomach. He was having trouble breathing properly and his eyes were blurry with salt water. The Professor extended his handkerchief and Marty used it to wipe his eyes and blow his nose. "I don't guess you're going to want this back," Marty said, an attempt at comedic deflection that didn't really work.

"When the paramedics arrived and took over, it was the first time it occurred to David to call me. He told me something terrible had happened and I needed to get home right away. By the time I arrived on the scene, three rescue workers were over Jane's body. My mind was in shock and denial. *This couldn't be happening. How did it happen?* David looked over at me, crestfallen, disheveled, and mouthed the word 'Ronny.'"

"When the paramedics pronounced her dead, I collapsed down beside Jane and wrapped her up in my arms. 'I love you so much. Please don't leave me,' I cried as I rocked her. I could see the hand prints on her neck where Ronny had strangled her. Other than that, she looked just like she had any other time I held her when she was sleeping. My brain refused the input it received. My heart felt as if it would explode. Air burned in my lungs. Panic set in. I knew she was gone, but another part of me rebelled. I placed her back down and frantically began administering CPR again until David came over and gently pulled me off her lifeless body. He stood me up and let me collapse into him. I wept on his shoulder."

The Professor watched Marty as he stared off into the distance. His mind was reliving the moment as if it were happening right then. As horrifying as the memory may be, he was now *able* to access it again, *able* to relive it. After a period of silence, the Professor probed Marty to continue the conversation. There was more to remember.

"And what of Ronny?"

"In the moments David was hunched over Jane administering CPR, Ronny went out onto the balcony of my third floor apartment and leapt off it. David had no idea where he had gone. In the rush to get to Jane nobody had noticed Ronny's body lying in the grass behind the building. By the time he was located and the emergency personnel found him, he was barely alive. He died in the ambulance on the way to the hospital."

The two men sat there for a long time, allowing the weight of all Marty said fill up the spaces between and around them. It was more than any one person should have to carry by himself. Marty should have at least had David. They shared this together. But David had been so traumatized by the event he couldn't speak of it, or even be reminded of it. After a few weeks, he left town, moved across the country to live with one of his cousins. He wouldn't respond to any of Marty's attempts to communicate with him. It was like they had never been friends at all. This added another layer of grief and guilt to Marty's ledger. He had put David through the hell of those moments and ruined their friendship in the process.

But perhaps Marty really wasn't to blame for that, either. Life is cruel and impossible sometimes, and maybe no one who gets caught in the wake of tragedy knows what to do or how to feel or why it happened.

The Professor brought Marty a bottle of water and the two of them sat there in silence while Marty continued to wipe away tears, attempting to regain his composure.

"I don't know what I would have done if I hadn't found you. As painful as it is to recall all of this, it doesn't compare to the uncertainty and sorrow I experienced when I was faced with losing all of my memories."

"There is a hard way to do things and an easy way. The easy way leads to strife and the hard way leads to freedom."

"You said that to me once before. At the bus stop?" Marty said, looking for confirmation.

The Professor nodded, a hint of a smile presenting across his lips.

Marty had so many questions, so many things left unanswered. He knew he'd never figure it all out. And maybe that was okay. But he did have a couple more questions he needed the answer to.

"If you were going to save the box, why require it of me in the first place?"

"Two reasons. First, I had to know you were completely committed. Only people at their breaking point will surrender what is most precious to them."

"And second?"

"If you did change your mind, you needed to work to get your memory back. Having access to those memory triggers would have been too easy. You couldn't be allowed to fix your situation so quickly."

"Why not?"

"You needed to know. To understand and feel, beyond doubt, how absolutely critical, how magnificent and necessary every memory and life experience is in shaping who we become. If you were going to get your memory back, you were going to have to choose to go down a difficult path. You had to choose the strenuous journey, the journey would lead you to freedom, to strength, to restoration."

"Then why did you leave the clues?"

"Ahh, the clues. Clues are a part of any discovery. There are clues everywhere to any and all mysteries if only you open your eyes and pay attention. And if there are clues…"

"…someone must have left those clues." Marty finished the Professor's thought, almost trance-like, stunned, amazed, overwhelmed by it all.

"The one who leaves the clues receives pleasure and enjoyment in creating a way for others to know and understand."

Marty nodded his head. It was making more sense to him now. The fact he had to want it, had to work for it, earn it. The thrill of the chase, the pursuit, the urgency of do or die. It had given him purpose, focus, a reason to live. It was the most difficult thing he had ever done. It was also the most exciting, the most worthwhile.

"Some people just stay with you. Long after they've gone. Over time, you might even begin to feel gratitude for your memories of Jane, for the fact that she impacted you so deeply you have reason to miss her." the Professor said, wrapping it all up.

The two men sat in silence for a long time, Marty trying to process all he had been through, everything he was learning about memory, about life, about himself.

"What happened to Ben?" Marty finally said, wondering about his one-time ally and friend.

"He's going to live, but he's got quite a bad injury to his hip. He'll never walk normally again. He's going to need help."

"Yeah. In more ways than one, I suppose." Marty let the implications sink into his bones.

"Is it too late for him? I mean, you know, to remember?"

"So long as he has breath, it's not too late for anything."

"You gave me my memory back. So you must be able to give him his memory back as well. But you won't unless he asks for it and believes it can be done." Marty said, understanding some things for the first time.

The Professor nodded gently.

"I'd like to see him, help him if I can. Maybe make him feel bad about the concussion he gave me."

"I think all of those things are wonderful ideas."

"I don't know how to find him."

"He's at Parkview Hospital. Room 4118."

Chapter Twenty-Two

"The earth laughs in flowers." - Ralph Waldo
Emerson

Trees moved past the windows of the truck Marty had borrowed from his brother-in-law as he made his way out of the city. He had briefly considered going straight to the hospital to check on Ben, but he knew there was somewhere he needed to go before he did anything else. It was a place he had only been once before, and the last time he was here it was so painful he doubled over with nausea, nearly passing out from the heartbreak.

As Marty turned into the property, past the matching Eternal Hills signs on either side of the entrance, he thought of how different things were this time around. The intense and piercing sadness was still there, and he knew it always would be. But underneath the sadness, bracing it and giving it balance, was a newfound peace which he could not explain or describe. There was a time when he wouldn't have thought it was possible. Even now, it seemed incongruous. But the things he could not put into words were holding his soul together just the same.

He drove the truck slowly around a curve and down a long straight section of road. He noticed a family under a green tent, saying their goodbyes to a loved one. His heart went out to them, and he wished each of them one day could have just a moment with the Professor to talk through their pain and loss. He wished for them to experience the same peace he now had.

May they find the Professor somewhere along life's road. And may they choose the difficult path that leads to healing.

It was the first time he prayed since he was a child.

When he reached the plots near the back of the cemetery, he pulled the truck over to the side and put it in park. Taking a deep breath, he got out of the truck and began walking toward the place where Jane's remains were laid to rest. Her mom had chosen to have her body cremated and her urn placed in a niche near her father's. There were no ashes in her father's niche because they never found his body, just a few small items that represented his life. A photo of him on a boat with his three children in his lap, a gold cross he occasionally wore around his neck, his high school football state championship ring.

The niches were buried in the ground as part of a rose garden, with bronze memorialization plaques on the top. Marty scanned the area until his eyes came upon her niche in the center of the bottom row.

Marianna Jane Carson

Beloved daughter, sister, friend.

Marty squatted down in front of the marker, just staring at the name, running his eyes over it for several minutes. *Marianna Jane Carson.* Tears were flowing down his cheeks in generous amounts, some coming to rest on the plaque. He reached down and began running his fingers across the raised letters of Jane's name.

I remember you.

He retrieved a tissue from one of his back pants pockets and wiped his nose with it. Then he sat down parallel to the plots, his arms over his knees. He felt he should talk to her, to say things to her as if she were right there. He didn't know where to begin. He looked over the plots of her and her father, and the empty one that would day would house her mother's remains, sweet Ava, and noticed a bouquet of beautiful roses.

"You once told me you loved me more than flowers. It was the most meaningful thing anyone's ever said to me because I knew just how much you loved them. It was such a joy to bring you a flower every Friday the years we were together, because I knew they were your favorite. Nobody had ever loved me more than their favorite thing in the world, or if they did, they never said it. But you said it. You were always saying things to re-shape my heart. I love you for that.

"I love how you loved your family, how you loved laughing and hugging and cuddling. I love how you loved the sound of the rain, how you loved to sing, especially when you would sing to me. You were so artistic - painting and writing poetry, always creating beautiful things. Yet you were so silly sometimes. Nobody could make me laugh like you, or could shock me and endear yourself to me at the same time like you did on a regular basis. You loved life, and you made me love and appreciate life in a way I never had before. You were this free spirit, independent and brave, adorable and strong.

"You were tender like a rose in full bloom, beautiful and soft, brilliant and fragile, a gift delivering warmth and joy to my life. Maybe that's why you loved flowers so much. You felt a kindred spirit with them. You were connected. You both brought so much vibrant color and beauty and artistry to the world.

You were like a flower.

Flowers were your favorite.

You loved me more than flowers."

Marty's voice grew softer with each of the last sentences until his voice faded completely. He reached into his pocket and pulled out another tissue, wiping the stream coming down both cheeks and then dabbing the corners of both eyes. After a few moments, he spoke once more.

"Despite my attempts to forget you, I couldn't. At least not completely. I've been dreaming of you. I wonder if one day I no longer will.

"I hope not. It's the only way I can spend time with you. Your presence inspires me, even if only when I sleep. I'm reminded of the night we spent under the stars on the lakeshore. As we lay there wrapped up in each other's arms looking up at the sky, you quoted W.B. Yeats. 'For the winds that awakened the stars are blowing through my blood.' I hang onto those words. Not only because they describe you perfectly, but because they describe what you did for me.

"You were the wind that awakened my soul. A part of you will always be running through my veins.

"I hope you can forgive me for wanting to forget you. I'll never walk away from your memory again. It will be with me, infusing my life with warmth, guiding me, providing joy to my heart, for as long as I live. Someday I hope to be able to express my gratitude for all you have done for me. You changed my life. In many ways, you saved me. I will spend the rest of my days doing my best to honor your spirit with the way I live. I love you, Jane Carson. You are the love of my life."

Marty stayed there for over an hour, just sitting with Jane. Thinking about her, loving her, remembering her.

Finally, when it was time, he pulled out a brand new lottery ticket from his front pocket and stood it up in the crack between the concrete and the top of Jane's plaque.

"Let me know if this is a winner and I'll drive to the next town and bring you another one."

He smiled at the memory, returned to the truck, and drove home.

Chapter Twenty-Three

"Forgiveness is the fragrance that the violet sheds on the heel that has crushed it." - Mark Twain

Marty went over his list yet again. Every bullet point scratched through but one. He went through each item, one by one. And he remembered them all. He relived them, awash with relief. All of the meaningful moments of his childhood, all of the shaping events of his upbringing, the innocent years, the awkward and thrilling teen years, graduations, firsts, lasts, passages, mistakes, achievements. He paused at each one, like pictures in an album, savoring them, brushing his hand over them, breathing them in.

He was sitting in a chair at Ben's bedside, waiting for him to wake up. He had been there for about an hour already. He had no idea what to expect when Ben woke up and saw him there. He wasn't sure what he would say, either. He had every right to be furious with Ben. The still-swollen spot on the top of his head was the easiest reason, and the most physically persistent reminder. But there were other reasons. Ben had deceived him from the start, had used him for his own nefarious purposes, had manipulated him and endangered his only opportunity to regain his memory, not to mention his life.

On the other hand, he never would have found the Professor without Ben's help. His knowledge of the Professor's house, his helpful insight into the workings of memory, his suggestion to keep the journal, motorized transportation, and the sheer comfort of knowing someone else in this world had made the same stupid decision he had made Marty realize he wasn't alone. That was Ben's real gift to Marty, whether he had ever salvaged his memory or not. So Marty chose to forgive. In a strange way, he understood Ben's actions, and in his position, he may have done the exact same thing. Without damaging another person's skull, if at all possible.

The nurse wouldn't tell Marty what, exactly, was the medical issue with Ben. Marty was anxious to find out what was wrong with his, er, friend. He wanted to see Ben, to express his forgiveness, to convince him to humble himself and ask for the Professor's help, to share with him everything he remembered about Jane, and about Ronny. He wanted Ben to know all of it. Maybe in seeing Marty's recovery, Ben might find some hope for his own one day. Ben had helped Marty find the Professor, even if it was for other motives. Marty swore to himself that he would do everything in his power to help Ben come back to the Professor some day as well.

A little over two hours after Marty had sat down at Ben's bedside, a nurse came in to check Ben's vitals, and the activity woke him. He slowly opened his eyes and smacked his lips together, remembering where he was, paying attention to the nurse, who at the moment was blocking Marty from Ben's view. After she checked his blood pressure, she moved to the other side of the bed, revealing Ben's visitor. The look of surprise on his face was real and yet it was not an antagonistic look. It was a *I can't believe you're here, why would you be here after what I've done* expression.

"Marty," Ben whispered, his strength still clearly eluding him. "What are you doing here? I'm so sorry, Marty. So sorry…" His voice trailed off as he closed his eyes and turned his head away. After a few minutes, the nurse left. Ben looked up to make sure they were alone in the room, then turned his head back away from Marty. "I never intended on hurting you physically. In the moment, rage just took over. I, I really don't know what happened. I'm not a violent person," he said, in the direction of the window.

"I know. And I forgive you."

"You forgive me?" Ben raised his head and looked directly at Marty, stunned. "How could you forgive me, just like that?"

"I put myself in your shoes. I really was able to see things from your perspective. And I think I can, better than anybody, understand where you were coming from. If it were me, I wouldn't have gone all Wyatt Earp on my head with the handle of your gun, but, to each his own." Marty hoped his casual and flippant summary of Ben's violence would let him know he was okay. That it was alright to joke about it. "Besides, this thing is healing up like a champ. The knot is barely even noticeable from space anymore."

Ben couldn't help but laugh. And he turned toward Marty, the shame and guilt seeming to relent a bit. "You're a better man than me.'

"Well, that's probably true. But I owe a lot to you. You gave me hope when I was running thin on the stuff. You were proof I wasn't alone. And even though you botched the whole thing, I was able to return to the Professor yesterday morning."

"You went back to that monster?"

"He's not a monster at all. And, yes, I did. He fixed me, Ben. He gave me my memory back. He could do the same for you, too."

"It's too late for me," Ben said, resigned. And before Marty could argue, he followed up with, "So what was it? What were you trying to forget? If you don't mind me asking."

Marty spent the next hour or so telling Ben the entire story he had shared with the Professor the day before. Ben only nodded off one time, but he apologized and Marty repeated the part he missed. Marty told him about Jane, about Ronny, the horror of it all. His feelings of extreme sorrow, guilt, and shame.

"I kept replaying the scene in my head," Marty said softly, tears gathering at the corner of his eyes again. "I would imagine Jane hearing the door open, expecting me, expecting love and warmth and finding terror instead. I would think about all of the plans I had made for that night. How differently it was supposed to go. The only thing greater than my sorrow over losing Jane was my feeling of personal responsibility for all of it. I tortured myself, consciously and subconsciously. The only thing worse than the waking hours were the nightmares. It was an endless cycle of pain and regret. I didn't see any way out."

"What did you do with the ring?" Ben asked, surprising Marty.

"I asked Jane's mom if the ring could be buried with her remains. After trying to convince me to sell it, she relented and said yes. I was going to spend the rest of my life with her," Marty finished, his words stretching out from his heart and lips into those places where all unfilled dreams float just beyond reach.

"I'm really sorry," Ben said, for what you've been through mentally and emotionally. For what I put you through physically."

"This?" Marty said, pointing to his head. "This was a piece of cake compared to all of that."

They both laughed, even though the mood in the room was still somber.

"You know, the Professor can help you remember, too."

"Maybe I don't *want* to remember," Ben said. "Maybe it's easier to blame someone else than overcome the past. Maybe my anger at the Professor was just a distraction to take my mind off my lack of courage in dealing with the choices I've made…

"Whatever the case, I'm just not ready. And I don't know if I ever will be," Ben finished.

"I understand," Marty said. "Just know I'm with you, no matter what. And if you ever decide you want to try and get your memory back, I'll take you there myself."

"On what, your one-seat bicycle?"

"I could get a tandem. We could do tandem. Or maybe we'll go in your VW bug, you riding shotgun for once."

Ben laughed and winced in pain. "Okay, enough about the Professor."

Marty, noticing the pain in Ben's face, used the opportunity to change the subject and find out what was going on with Ben.

"So what's the story? You haven't told me your prognosis. It's clear you're in a lot of pain."

"Yeah, it hurts pretty good. They've got me on some really strong pain meds, and I have this button I can push whenever it gets bad. Doesn't happen as often now."

"What hurts?"

"My hip. Got a bullet lodged in there. Doc says it's in a spot where they can't get it out. I'll have it as a souvenir for the rest of my life. And I'll never walk normally again. Says I could improve with physical therapy, but I'll have a pronounced limp until the day I die. A daily reminder of my folly."

"I'm sorry, man. I really am. I heard the gun go off, and I saw one of you fall. But I didn't know which one of you went down."

"And you wanted it to be me, I'm sure."

Marty didn't say anything.

"It's ok. I get it. I had just cracked your skull. I would've been cheering against me, too."

"Where are you going when you get out of here? I don't think you'll be able to live by yourself for a while."

"I really hadn't thought it through. I'll think of something."

"Well, I have an extra bedroom. You should come and stay with me for a while. You won't be able to operate the clutch on your VW for some time. I could drive you to physical therapy, cook for us, help you in any way you want me to. Just until you get yourself up and going. What do you say?"

"I say you're crazy to ask your attacker to be your roommate. But I'm kind of crazy, too. And 'birds of a feather flock together,' they say. I think I'll take you up on that offer, my friend. So long as you don't mind my affinity for bourbon and cigars."

"I'll cope somehow." Marty said. Then followed up with, "This could be a beautiful friendship."

"If you were trying to do *Casablanca*, you said it wrong."

"Well, you're name's not Louie, either. It was close enough."

"I could be a Louie," Ben said, as Marty sat there shaking his head and laughing.

Chapter Twenty-Four

"Joy always comes after pain." - Guillaume
Apollinaire

A few days later, Marty was back at the hospital. Ben was being released. He had been busy back at his apartment preparing the spare bedroom and doing general clean up for Ben's arrival. He was kind of excited about having a roommate again.

Ben was sitting in a wheelchair in his room, waiting for Marty to wheel him out.

"How you feeling, big guy?" Marty asked, tossing him a Red Delicious apple.

"I'm alright. Ready to get out of this place, that's for sure." Ben said, catching the apple and nodding his head to say thank you. He took a big juicy bite and smiled at Marty, as if to say *You know me well.*

"Well, what are we waiting for?" Marty continued.

"You, actually. I was waiting for you." Ben teased. "Been sitting in this damn chair for about thirty minutes now. All dressed up and no place to go."

"Yeah, um, sorry about that. I was doing some last minute clean up at the house and I lost track of time."

"At least you didn't *forget* me."

Marty stared at Ben for a second in mock indignation and then started laughing.

"You're more likely to forget me, remember?" Marty shot back.

"Right. Who are you again?"

"Your new Roomie, that's who. Also, your new Landlord. You got first and last month's rent ready?" Marty said as he stepped behind the wheelchair and began to wheel Ben out of the room.

"I was kind of relying on my charm and wit to carry me for a while."

"That'll get you about three days."

Marty rolled Ben down the corridor to the elevators and punched the down button. They stood there in silence for a few moments, both watching the light indicator move from one all the way up to four. The elevator dinged and Marty moved Ben into position. As the door opened, Marty locked eyes with the only passenger on the elevator. It was the same eyes he had seen a few days before. The eyes that had haunted him in his dreams ever since. He knew now who they belonged to. He remembered.

"Joy." Marty said.

"Hey Marty." Joy responded cautiously, still remembering their bizarre encounter. "You're going to act like you know me now?"

"I, I can't explain that. Just know I'm sorry. I was under a lot of stress and in a terrible hurry that day. And that's all I really know to say. I hope you'll forgive me."

"Of course I do. You know I love you. We share a bond that can never be broken. You loved my sister as much or more than I did."

"This is my friend Ben." Marty said, changing the subject.

"It's nice to meet you, Ben."

Ben smiled widely, nodded his head, and backed his wheelchair up a few feet, giving Marty and Joy space to talk.

"It's crazy running into you again." Joy began.

"Yeah, I know, right?" *I was just picking up my friend Ben, here. One minute sooner or one minute later and we would have missed each other completely.* "You work here now?" Marty asked, nodding toward her clothing, which consisted of nursing scrubs and Crocs.

"I do. Just started this week, actually. I finished nursing school in the fall, did some traveling, and now here I am."

"Well, congratulations. I'm really proud of you." Marty tried to control his eye contact. Joy was one of those people who just laser-locked eyes when you were talking to her.

"I'd love to catch up sometime, hear about your travels."

"That sounds nice, Marty. I'd really like that." Marty let the eye contact linger for a little bit too long and he felt something in the pit of his stomach. *What is going on here?*

"Well, I don't want to keep my friend waiting. Need to get him home so he can rest. Can I call you sometime?"

"I'd like that. Here's my number," Joy said, scribbling down on the corner of one of the papers she was holding, then tearing it off and handing it to Marty.

Marty took it, then instinctively leaned in to give her a hug. "So good to see you," Joy said softly into Marty's ear,